THE ANGRY DEAD

BY

ROSEMARY PARDOE

CATHAVEN PRESS

THE ANGRY DEAD
(Occult Detective Magazine Special #1)
by Rosemary Pardoe

ISBN: 978-1-9160212-3-5

Publishers: Jilly Paddock & Dave Brzeski (as Cathaven Press)

http://greydogtales.com/blog/occult-detective-magazine/theangrydead/
occultdetectivemagazine@gmail.com

Editor: Dave Brzeski

Interior design by Dave Brzeski and Jilly Paddock

Published by
Cathaven Press,
Peterborough,
United Kingdom
cathaven.press@cathaven.co.uk

Early versions of these stories previously appeared as by Mary Ann Allen in the following publications:

Abbreviations:

The Angry Dead (Crimson Altar, 1986): AD1

The Angry Dead (Richard Fawcett, 2000): AD2

'*The Gravedigger and Death*': AD1, AD2, *Ghosts & Scholars #5* (1983), *Tales by Moonlight Vol II* (Salmonson ed., 1989)

'*Hold Fast*': AD1, AD2, *Dark Dreams 2* (Dempsey & Cowperthwaite ed., Spring 1985)

'*Joan*': AD1, AD2, *Tales by Moonlight* (Salmonson ed., 1983, 1985)

'*Joan*' (Revised Version): *Occult Detective Magazine #0* (Brzeski & Linwood Grant ed., 2021)

'*Annie's Ghost*' (retitling of '*Annie and the Anchorite*'): AD1, AD2

'*Margaret and Catherine*': AD1, AD2, *A Graven Image* (Haunted Library 1985)

'*Ne Resurgat*': AD1, AD2, *A Graven Image* (Haunted Library 1985)

'*The Blue Boar of Totenhoe*': AD1, AD2, *Fantasy & Terror #3* (Salmonson, 1984)

'*The Chauffeur*': AD1, AD2, *The Virago Book of Ghost Stories Vol II: The Twentieth Century* (Dalby ed, 1991, plus various later editions under different titles)

'*The Hatchment*': AD1, AD2, *Fantasy & Terror #1* (Salmonson, 1984)

'*The Wandlebury Eyecatcher*': AD1, AD2, *Fantasy Macabre #6* (Salmonson, 1985)

'*The Sheelagh-na-gig*': AD2, *Midnight Never Comes* (Rodens ed, 1997), *The Black Veil and Other Tales of Supernatural Sleuths* (Valentine ed, 2008)

'*The Cambridge Beast*': AD2, *Dark Dreams #6* (Dempsey & Cowperthwaite, 1988)

All stories have been newly revised by the author, and with the exception of '*Joan*', are original to this collection.

ABOUT THE AUTHOR

Rosemary Pardoe was the editor of *Ghosts & Scholars* magazine from 1979 to 2019. She has edited five *Ghosts & Scholars Books of...* for Sarob Press, most recently *The Ghosts & Scholars Book of Mazes* (2020). *The Ghosts & Scholars Book of Follies and Grottoes* will be published in 2022. A collection of her articles and essays, *The Black Pilgrimage and Other Explorations*, was published by Shadow Publishing in 2018. The stories in *The Angry Dead* are her only fiction.

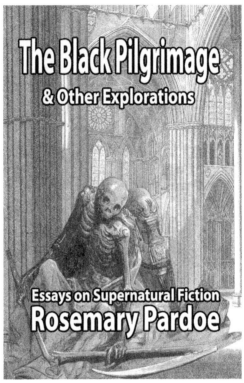

INTRODUCTION

"But these precautions avail little against the angry dead"
(*M.R. James*, 'The Malice of Inanimate Objects')

I can remember exactly *where* I was when I got the idea for the first of the twelve stories which were eventually collected together in *The Angry Dead*, published by Richard Fawcett in 2000. I was at Euston Station about to get on a train to go home from London to Liverpool, and suddenly an ending came into my head, which I thought was pretty original. I still do—it's the climax of '*The Sheelagh-na-gig*'. I then wrote the story (including some opinions on the nature of sheelagh-na-gigs which I've long since abandoned!). I was not happy with it, and put it away, showing it only to David Rowlands, then assistant editor (fiction) on my M.R. Jamesian small press zine *Ghosts & Scholars*. Unlike all the tales which followed, it was written in the third rather than the first person. Eventually I threw the manuscript away (this was before I got a computer and became quite OCD on backing up). Next came several stories in a rush and I can't remember in which order I wrote them. All I do

1

recall is that I seemed to produce one every few weeks for a period of several months in the 1980s. If I'd kept up this schedule I could be today's Lionel Fanthorpe (who wrote a total of 381 tales for *Supernatural Stories* in the '50s and '60s)! But no, the urge to write fiction left me as suddenly as it had arrived, and it has never really returned.

From 1983 to 1985, stories appeared in small press zines: Jeff Dempsey and David Cowperthwaite's *Dark Dreams* ('Hold Fast'), Jessica Amanda Salmonson's *Fantasy & Terror* ('*The Blue Boar of Totenhoe*', '*The Hatchment*') and *Fantasy Macabre* ('*The Wandlebury Eyecatcher*'); and in Jessica's two *Tales by Moonlight* books ('*Joan*', '*The Gravedigger and Death*'). It's less the case now, but back then I was a little wary of editors including their own stories in collections, which is why I was unsure about putting any of them in *Ghosts & Scholars* until David Rowlands jokingly gave me an ultimatum: either I put '*The Gravedigger and Death*' into *G&S*, or he wouldn't let me publish his Father O'Connor tale '*Conkers*'. So both went into *G&S #5* (1983), to be followed by two stories in the 1985 Haunted Library booklet *A Graven Image* ('*Ne Resurgat*' and '*Margaret and Catherine*', with two more by David and two by Roger Johnson). The Haunted Library was my imprint for single-author and single-topic booklets, and in this case all of the contents had Essex settings. I decided I would slightly disguise my identity with the Mary Ann Allen pseudonym (part of my two forenames plus my maternal surname), but it was never anything other than an open secret.

In 1986, Jeff Dempsey and David Cowperthwaite's Crimson Altar Press published *The Angry Dead*, a booklet containing ten of Mary Ann Allen's stories along with an introduction by me under my own name, explaining that Mary Ann was something of a "mysterious, reclusive figure", and couldn't be persuaded to compose her own foreword. The two missing tales were *'The Sheelagh-na-gig'*, and the night climbing story *'The Cambridge Beast'* (both, incidentally, displaying my love of apocalypses). All of the stories apart from *'The Cambridge Beast'* featured the church restorer Jane Bradshawe, who seemed to encounter the supernatural not just in ecclesiastical buildings but all over the place! Several of Jane's experiences were inspired by my interest in such things as inn signs and follies (*'The Blue Boar of Totenhoe'*, *'The Wandlebury Eyecatcher'*); others by places I'd visited (Cotehele House in Cornwall is the thinly disguised setting for *'The Chauffeur'*, which is based on a genuine haunting); and one or two on my particular knowledge of certain types of church furnishings. As I explain in the booklet introduction, concerning Mary Ann (i.e. me!):

> Outside the supernatural genre her only writings have been on the rather esoteric subject of Royal Coats of Arms in Churches... Royal Arms (and the related, but even more esoteric subject of Commonwealth Arms) feature prominently in one story, *'Hold Fast'*, and peripherally in another, *'Joan'*. The former was inspired by the discovery of a

Commonwealth Arms—every bit as rare as described—in Ramsey, Essex, and its subsequent restoration. I'm told, though, that in real life nothing untoward has resulted from the arms being re-erected in the church. The letter quoted in the story is based on an authentic one sent to Hertfordshire churches.

'*The Gravedigger and Death*' was inspired by a fragmentary wall-painting at Yaxley church in Huntingdonshire. The Reverend Sir Adam Gordon, mentioned in the story, really did exist and was rector of West Tilbury (alias West Tilford) at the beginning of the nineteenth century, although his local history book is entirely fictional. For further information on him, see my article, '*A Hertfordshire Church's Memorial for a "Mad" King*', in *Hertfordshire Countryside*, November 1975.

In '*Margaret and Catherine*', Crossley Abbey is Waltham Abbey in Essex, and the Bisham Tomb is based on the Denny Tomb there. My description in the story is fairly close to the real thing: "a large Tudor tomb with reclining life-size figures of a lady and gentleman". On a panel along the front is:

> ... a row of praying offspring... Of the five daughters shown, three were kneeling modestly in their Elizabethan caps and ruffs, but the fourth had half-turned to look at the fifth and smallest who was tugging at her sleeve and obviously trying to draw her away from her devotions.

What was the mystery of that fifth figure? The story explains it as far as the Bisham Tomb is concerned, but the panel on the real Denny Tomb is much as described except that there are six boys on one side as well as the (four) figures on the distaff side, and the smallest of the latter is actually a boy and not a girl. The littlest girl and the boy were apparently twins, which accounts for their being together, but there is surely more to it than that. *Is* the boy pulling on his sister's arm, causing her to turn slightly, or is she leading him? What the full story behind the unusual pose is, I've yet to discover (the twins didn't die young).

The later, out-rider of my stories, '*The Cambridge Beast*', was written a couple of years after the booklet and was published by Jeff and David in *Dark Dreams 6* (1988). In 1991, '*The Chauffeur*' was reprinted by Richard Dalby in *The Virago Book of Ghost Stories, Volume II*.

After this, every so often, someone would try encouraging me to write a new Jane Bradshawe tale. It wasn't going to happen! But then Barbara and Christopher Roden asked if I'd do something for their 1997 Ash-Tree Press anthology, *Midnight Never Comes*. Ruefully, I remembered '*The Sheelagh-na-gig*', thinking that it was a shame I'd disposed of my copy—it might have deserved rescuing, if only for that original climax. I mentioned this to David Rowlands, and miraculously it turned out that he'd kept the hard copy I'd sent him. So, with some revision, it appeared in the Ash-Tree book (and was, incidentally, reprinted by Mark Valentine in *The Black Veil* in 2008). The first Mary Ann Allen story to be written was thus the last to see print. At some point before publication, I altered it from third to first person and also toned down the dubious fertility goddess explanation for the sheelagh-na-gig—I've done more of that in the latest revision, without, I hope, lessening the impact of the ending (described by Glen Hirshberg in a review as "subtle, sensual and unnerving"!).

Richard Fawcett and Jessica Amanda Salmonson started a short-lived publishing project around the turn of the century—most notably, perhaps, they reprinted all of Augustus Jessopp's supernatural short stories in *The Phantom Coach and Other Ghost Stories of an Antiquary*. I never did really understand why Jessica liked my stories so much, but she did, and finally the result in 2000 was a nice little book from Richard Fawcett, reprinting all twelve of them together for the first time, and illustrated by Wendy Wees. Meanwhile, Jane Bradshawe had been turning up elsewhere. In David Rowlands' above-mentioned '*Conkers*', she quite literally trips over Fr O'Connor. As the good Father tells it:

> I... entered the cool interior of the church... I fear I am getting rather deaf, and received ample confirmation of the fact. In stopping to make arthritic obeisance to the altar, I had not heard the young lady following close on my heels; with the result that she shot headlong over my sprawled feet, making a clatter with a galvanised bucket and uttering some exclamation that also evaded me. I helped her up, with due apologies... She told

me, speaking clearly, that she was an artist specialising in church restoration work, and had been summoned hither by the Diocesan authority to inspect the condition of the wall-painting over the chancel arch.

And in Jessica Amanda Salmonson's own tales concerning her paranormal investigator Penelope Pettiweather (first published in her Haunted Library booklet *Harmless Ghosts*[1]), it turned out that Penelope was a regular correspondent of Jane's.

So there the history of the not-very mysterious Mary Ann Allen might have ended but now, thanks to the powers-that-be at *Occult Detective Magazine*, her stories have a fresh lease of life. For this new edition of *The Angry Dead*, I've completely revised all twelve of the stories, making substantial changes and also retitling one, because I thought that the original title gave part of the plot away (never a good thing). I'm afraid there's still no hope of any new stories though!

--- Rosemary Pardoe

[1] Jessica Amanda Salmonson's Penelope Pettiweather tales have since been collected in *The Complete Weird Epistles of Penelope Pettiweather, Ghost Hunter* (Alchemy Press 2016).

Available from The Alchemy Press

Jessica Amanda Salmonson's
The Complete Weird Epistles of
Penelope Pettiweather

GHOST HUNTER

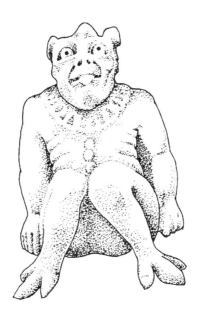

THE GRAVEDIGGER AND DEATH

South Tilford on the Essex Marshes is one of the most atmospheric places in the county, and as I walked up the gravel path toward St Peter's Church I found it hard to believe that I was still in the twentieth century. With the tall, grey medieval building ahead of me, the equally grey 1860s Coal Fort in the near distance, and the dark, lowering sky above, I would not have been surprised to find, on looking around, that my small red car—which was parked by the gate—had been transformed into a horse-drawn carriage.

My name is Jane Bradshawe and I'm a church restorer. I was in South Tilford to look at some seventeenth-century wall-paintings in St Peter's, and to decide whether they could be cleaned without suffering damage. The rector, I knew, should be waiting for me inside, but when I first opened the heavy door, the building appeared empty. Then I heard a movement up at the east end and spotted a tubby, balding figure attending to a censer.

I have nothing against High Church Anglicans, but they do seem to pick the most cloyingly heavy incense; the sort which is guaranteed to give me a headache in minutes. The scent which filled this church was no exception.

Not a good start to the visit, I thought; but Father Cranage, who came hurrying down the chancel—hand outstretched—as soon as he saw me, was such a sweet old fellow that I couldn't stay irritated. He led me to the west wall, on which the paintings sheltered beneath a layer of grime and peeling whitewash.

"You see, my dear, there are two figures—one on each side of the door. They're hard to make out now, but I understand that authorities such as the *Victoria County History* believe them to be a gravedigger and Death."

Although the restoration job would be dirty and difficult, I soon saw that it would probably be rewarding. "These are quite rare," I said. "There are similar figures in a church in Huntingdonshire, but they're badly defaced. It would be exciting if yours were in better condition."

"Yes, indeed," the rector nodded. "Although, curiously enough, a few of my parishioners have hinted to me that the paintings should be left alone. I've been here for forty years now, and I hope they have learned to trust me, but no one has been able to tell me *why* they believe the work shouldn't be done. I don't think they know themselves."

Later that evening, after the long drive back to my little house in Northamptonshire, I wrote my report for the Diocesan Advisory Committee, recommending that the restoration be carried out, and that I would like to do it.

* * *

A couple of weeks afterwards I was in Essex again, on another job, trying in vain to rescue a hatchment which had been crudely repainted by a well-meaning parishioner in the mistaken belief that he was 'restoring' it. Before returning home, I decided to spend a day in the Essex Record Office, finding out what I could about South Tilford church. Searching through old, handwritten churchwardens' accounts and similar documents is a task I hate. It's hard, eye-straining work and, more often than not, it produces no results whatsoever. My luck seemed to be out on this day. I could find no information on the history of the wall-paintings or their unknown artist.

Serendipity is something which all researchers experience from time to time. It causes the very piece of knowledge for which you've been looking to fall into your hands, usually from a totally unexpected source, just as you've given up hope of ever finding it. This was what happened when, despairing of the church records, I started to browse through the printed books in the Record Office library. For no obvious reason, I picked up a small, dowdy green volume without a title on the spine. It proved to be *The History and Lore of the Villages of the Essex Marshes* by the Reverend Sir Adam Gordon who was, it seemed, the rector of West Tilford, the adjoining parish to South Tilford, during the early years of the nineteenth century. Turning quickly to the short chapter on South Tilford, I found a section on the wall-paintings. What Gordon had to say about them was highly intriguing:

> *"On the west wall [of the church] are two paintings, of a gravedigger and a skeleton. The traditional reason for the making of them is fast being forgotten by the villagers, so I am pleased to be able to record it here. It is said that the gravedigger was one Meshach Leach, sexton of the parish during the first part of the seventeenth century. There was a new incumbent at this time and he instructed Leach to remove an old stone from the churchyard. This object was held in heathen awe by the local people and was therefore a source of disgust to the rector. Leach protested very strongly, but he could not refuse for fear of losing his position, so he finally gave way. No one could be persuaded to help him, but unluckily the stone was small enough for him to move unaided, and the rector made a point of overseeing the task until completed. From that day the sexton was hounded by a figure which came to be called the 'guardian'. No clear description*

is now available, but there are hints of its being skeletal and extremely unpleasant to look upon.

"Three weeks later the vengeful creature pursued the unhappy man even into the very church itself, and it was there that the rector discovered poor Leach, apparently dead of an apoplexy. The rector was then much troubled in his sleep and finally had the stone replaced. He commissioned Meshach's brother, Shadrach, a sign painter, to produce the figures we see today, as a warning to future incumbents.

"I cannot tell how much of this strange story is true and how much romance, but the old stone does indeed exist, and can still be seen in South Tilford churchyard, a few yards from the main path to the south door. I find myself unable to believe that a servant of Satan such as this 'guardian' could have chased the unfortunate Leach into the sanctuary of a House of God. If the basic tale be true, I would suggest that the sexton injured himself when lifting the stone, causing brain-fever and hallucinations which led inevitably to his death."

I made a mental note (as a point of interest only, of course) to check whether the stone still existed, when I had the chance.

* * *

The opportunity came a month later, at the beginning of February, when I received the go-ahead from the Diocesan Advisory Committee, and arranged with Father Cranage to stay in his spare room at the rectory for the next few weeks. I knew I was in for a long, messy job, but hopefully with a final result which would make all the effort worthwhile.

The Essex Marshes are at their most timeless in the dark months of January and February. My feeling of no longer being in the twentieth century returned as I drove up to the church, and increased when I glanced over to the Thames on my right, and saw a distant line of tall ships' masts moving gracefully by. It was a race, of course, but for a brief moment I wondered whether this was the invasion that the Coal Fort had been built to defend the country against. Before driving on to the rectory, I parked the Mini and slipped into the graveyard to look for the mysterious stone. Sure enough, it was in the position which Reverend Gordon had described. I must admit to a slight feeling of relief.

Father Cranage was as jovial as ever. His house was a large and slightly decaying eighteenth-century building, but he was sensibly using only a small part of it, which was cluttered with his many possessions (including, I noted with approval, a fine little model railway layout), and exuded the same air of gentle friendliness as the rector himself. As he showed me to the airy spare room, which would be my bedroom, he admitted apologetically that it had been prepared in a hurry by himself. He explained that his 'daily', Mrs Coggins, was laid up 'with her legs', and so we would have to rough it. Since Mrs Coggins' daughter was to bring in a hot meal for us every evening, it seemed like fairly luxurious 'roughing it' to me.

The next day a group of local men helped me to put up a scaffolding platform in the church, and of course I paid them in the traditional way—with money for beer! The platform needed to be no more than four feet from the ground, which was a relief to me as I dislike heights. I started on the right-hand figure—that of the gravedigger—and work progressed splendidly. Two weeks later, 'Meshach' was revealed. Despite some slight damage, his general condition was excellent.

I had told Father Cranage the story of the figures, and we both noticed that the drab brown-clad sexton had a scared and pathetically unhappy look.

"Poor old soul," said the rector, as we stood admiring my efforts, late one afternoon. "I do hope the tale isn't true."

I agreed. "Perhaps," I suggested, "the whole thing was invented in order to explain his sad expression."

"I hope so, I do indeed. It is a shame that our Parish Registers survive only from the middle of the seventeenth century—probably too late for them to include the death of Meshach if it really did happen."

I nodded, but then something occurred to me. "*Meshach* Leach, if he existed, may have died too early, but this need not be the case with his brother Shadrach, who supposedly painted the wall. If we can find him in your records at least it will prove that the family was real."

We hurried to the vestry where, fortunately, the documents were being readied for loan to the Record Office, and were therefore in good order. It was a fairly simple matter to work through the list of deaths, and a few minutes later, under May 7th 1672, we found the entry we wanted. It read:

Shadrak Leche, aged 73 years, son of John and Azuba, brother of Meshak.

"Well," I said, leaning back in my chair to look at the rector, "we know now that there is *some* truth in the story, and that Meshach existed."

"I shall pray for him," said the good Father.

* * *

It was when I began cleaning the figure of Death that my keenness started to evaporate. During the daylight hours nothing untoward happened, but February days are so short that I had to continue working after dusk had fallen. When it was really dark I switched on the electric lights in the church, but I don't like using artificial light if I can avoid it, so I tended to work in the dusk for as long as I could. In the hour or so when the setting sun was throwing disconcerting shadows behind the furnishings, I found that I was becoming increasingly troubled. I have been in so many churches in the years since leaving art school that the shadows and noises, which they all contain, don't trouble me at all; but the *physical* discomfort I felt at South Tilford was unique in my experience. First the smell of incense became oppressive and intense, and naturally my head began to ache; and then the building started to feel uncomfortably hot. The old Gurney's Patent Boiler, against the north wall, heated the church very efficiently, but the temperature at this time of year should rarely have risen above sixty degrees. Now, in the evenings, it was rising into the nineties and making me feel positively faint.

I might have doubted the evidence of my own senses had it not been for the fact that Father Cranage noticed it too, during his frequent visits to see how I was getting on. He called in a man to look at the boiler in case it was malfunctioning, but no fault could be found. The puzzle remained, and it was evident that the oppressiveness was slightly worse each day; consequently my headaches became harder and harder to shake off.

To add to this, neither I nor the Father liked the look of the second figure which my careful cleaning was revealing. It was not the ordinary skeleton I had been expecting, but something altogether more grotesque, although it was certainly skeletal enough. From its bones hung shreds of what might have been cloth, or flesh, and the sardonically smiling face was undoubtedly fleshed, with parchment-like skin drawn tight against the skull. If this exceedingly unpleasant creation was intended to portray Death then the artist must have wanted the congregation to fear their final hour with a frightening intensity. If, on the other hand, it *was* the guardian of the story then I felt very glad that the stone in the churchyard was still in position.

By early March, my work was nearing completion, much to my relief. During my final evening in the church, the oppression was worse than ever. "Another night like this," I thought to myself, "and I'll be in danger of fainting and falling off the platform. A broken ankle is all I need."

As I turned to climb down and switch off the lights, I caught a movement out of the corner of my eye. Had the huddled shadow behind the boiler moved? I had no time to decide before another shadow, this one definitely moving, detached itself from the gloom of the chancel and started to make its way jerkily down the church. Its motion reminded me incongruously of a child playing hopscotch, but this was no child. It was tall, bony and impossibly thin—perhaps I can best describe it as a huge and humanoid stick insect. As it approached the patch of darkness behind the boiler, which now seemed to resemble a cowering figure, it reached out its hideous arms and the two shadows met, and merged. I heard—inside my head—a terrible, hopeless scream; and then there was silence. They were gone, leaving only a slight, distasteful smell of mould in my nostrils, which the scent of incense quickly overpowered.

I realised that I was clinging on for dear life to an upright on the scaffolding, otherwise I would certainly have fallen. But not for a moment had I felt threatened by the manifestation which I had just seen. When the shadow was making its way towards the boiler, it was also coming in my direction, but I knew that I was not its object, and that it could not harm me. I was merely seeing a re-enactment of that which had gone before.

* * *

If wall-paintings are in bad condition, restorers can suggest that they be concealed beneath a layer of whitewash to protect them. The figures at South Tilford didn't need this treatment, but I recommended it anyway, and although I did not tell Father Cranage my real reasons, he was happy to agree. "I'm afraid the older members of my congregation are being frightened by the grim reaper there," he said, "and even threatening not to come to my services." So, with the permission of the Diocesan Authorities, the paintings were covered up.

As I see it, there is no actual danger as long as the stone remains in position in the graveyard, but I believe that by revealing their images, I re-awakened the *shades* of the 'guardian' and of poor Meshach Leach. I suspect they also haunted the church when the paintings were new, which would account for several attempts made in the following centuries to deface and hide them. Ironically they were thereby preserved in much better condition than most contemporary work of a similar nature. By covering them up again, I hope I have 'laid' the shades, at least for the time being. Whether I took this action from pity for the unquiet spirit of the sexton, or for fear of the other, I will leave you to decide.

"One of the finest practitioners of dark fiction of our times."

"Somewhere between Lovecraft and Ligotti, grounded but scrabbling in the darkness, bringing forth glittering treasures from the shadowed places."

"Clearly demonstrates his mastery of the weird in a breathtaking array of stories that can't be neatly categorized but are nevertheless wonderful... Highly recommended."

WHERE ALL IS NIGHT, AND STARLESS

BY JOHN LINWOOD GRANT

5 Star reviews across all platforms.
Paperbacks from Amazon.
E-formats from Journalstone.

where all is night,
and starless

john linwood grant

CABROL

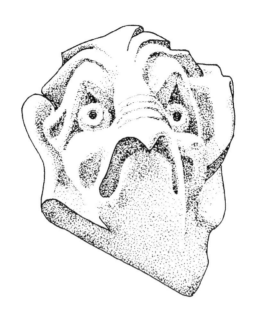

HOLD FAST

The job I had been asked to do at Marston church, in the north-east corner of Essex, was strictly routine: the reframing of a good, late Stuart Royal Coat of Arms. So when, with the aid of a sturdy parishioner and a step-ladder, I got the painting down from its position on the west wall, it was with some surprise that I discovered another shield, crudely painted on the reverse of the wooden board. I make no claim to any expertise in heraldic matters, but I recognised the quarterings immediately: the crosses of St George and St Andrew, and the Irish Harp. Here was an example of the Arms of the Commonwealth, which were put up in some churches in the middle of the seventeenth century, to replace the Royal Arms that Oliver Cromwell had ordered to be destroyed when he became Lord Protector. At the Restoration in 1660, such shields were taken down and the Royal Arms returned to their customary place, where they marked the monarch's position as Head of the Church of England, as they had done since the reign of Henry the Eighth. So extant examples of the Commonwealth Arms in churches are rare, practically to the point of non-existence. Only one other was known to me then—at North Walsham in Norfolk—and I have since been unable to discover any more.

Of course, the rector and his wife had to be summoned quickly and the importance of my discovery explained to them. I strongly recommended that an attempt be made to restore the shield, which was in very bad condition having been left facing the wall for centuries. I can't say that the Reverend Plymtree was as excited about my find as I had hoped, but perhaps this was natural since he was very much the High Church man, as the unfortunate series of modern 'Stations of the Cross' around the walls indicated. He seemed all for my finishing the reframing and leaving matters as they were. Reluctantly this is what I did, but when I returned home I set about informing the appropriate authorities, and was soon able to secure the promise of a grant for the restoration work. On those terms, the rector could hardly refuse my offer to do the job, and a few weeks later I was back in the parish, fully prepared for the challenging task.

The village of Marston is an attractive one, unspoiled by the caravan sites and ramshackle bungalows which cluster around the coastal towns, yet far enough away from Colchester to avoid ever becoming just another suburb. I was to lodge with the churchwarden, a Mr Johnson, in his cottage halfway down the pretty, tree-lined lane leading to the church. This was a very satisfactory arrangement as far as I was concerned, and much preferable to staying in the rectory; a large modern house apparently filled to the rafters with children of assorted sexes and animals of unexpected variety.

Mr Johnson was a quiet widower in his early sixties, whose single and time-consuming hobby was charting the history of the village. After sitting me down and pouring out a cup of tea, he launched straight into his favourite subject.

"I have been going through the church records, and have found a copy of something which should certainly interest you, Miss Bradshawe. It is here in my desk..."

There followed a rather lengthy silence, broken only by the rustle of papers as he sorted through the various cubicles and drawers of his bureau. Clearly he was not yet used to doing his own tidying up! At last the missing item was found, entangled in an old electricity bill, and Mr Johnson proudly presented it to me.

"It's a letter," he said, "which was sent to the minister and churchwardens of Marston in 1650. For some reason one of the churchwardens, Mr Joseph Gill, copied it into his accounts of that year, so it has been preserved."

I took the typed sheet and read:

Gentlemen,
We are informed that in your church there

*remaynes standinge the Arms of the late
King, which have been ordered to be taken
away in other publique places.*

*We therefore desire you to destroye the
said Arms and put up the State's Arms in
their place, and that you certifie the
councell of your proceedings herein before
the last instant of December.*

The letter was signed on behalf of the
Commissioners for the Militia of the County of
Essex, and dated December lst, 1650.

When I had finished, Mr Johnson took the
paper from me, and stared at it pensively.

"I think this, on top of the King's execution the
previous year, broke Joseph Gill's heart, for it's
clear from his notes in the Account Books that he
was a staunch King's man. After the letter there is
an angry scrawl in his hand, which I have made out
to read, 'Not while I yet live'; and it does seem that
Gill succeeded in keeping the Commonwealth
Arms out of the church till his death only three
months later. It was not until late in 1651 that the
records show a payment—I think it was of fourteen
shillings and sixpence—for their erection.
Unfortunately the artist is not named."

As he got up to show me to my room, Mr
Johnson added, "I'm so sorry that I don't have the
original churchwardens' accounts here, but they're
away being copied for the Record Office at the
moment. At least you might like to see old Gill's
memorial tablet tomorrow. It's in the south aisle of
the church, under a mat. If you have a spare
minute, do take a look at it."

I promised that I would.

* * *

The next morning dawned dull and wet, and as I shook the raindrops from my jacket in the sanctuary of the church porch, I remembered my promise. Knowing that I was quite likely to forget it again, I went straight to the south aisle before unpacking my equipment box.

The memorial slab, which I found near the east end, was a typical example of mid-seventeenth-century craftsmanship: plain to the point of starkness and with just a short biblical inscription:

> *Prove all things; hold fast that which is good. 1 Thess. V.21*

It seemed a suitable monument to the old man's steadfastness, right or wrong.

Time passed quickly during the following hours, as I got down to work on the remains of the ancient shield. My intention was to preserve the remnants rather than filling in the gaps with new paint, and this required a good deal of concentration. Unfortunately I was disturbed at frequent intervals by a sparrow which had become trapped in the church and was flapping hysterically around the roof beams. Occasionally it swooped down to the ground and I would catch sight of it out of the corner of my eye. Once or twice I had the feeling that a much larger body was there as well—it occurred to me that a cat or dog might have followed me into the building without my noticing.

On one occasion I turned suddenly, convinced that something big and unpleasant was dodging about close by, only to see it resolve itself into a perfectly innocuous—and stationary—bench-end. "Eye-strain! Maybe I need a holiday," I muttered, determined to ignore all further interruptions.

It was nearly tea-time when I thought I heard a faint grating noise in the body of the church, and a few seconds later, I was certain of the slow and laboured footsteps which approached from the same direction. Being in the middle of an awkward manoeuvre involving a flaking section of paintwork, I didn't stop to see who it was. "If they want me," I reasoned, "they'll speak up. And if they've just come to watch, they're welcome."

After a minute or two it dawned on me that I had not heard the church door open, and at the same time my uneasy feeling of earlier in the day returned. The steps had stopped just behind me, and then there was a voice, apparently only inches from my ear, although I felt no breath or movement of air. Painfully, and it seemed with terrible effort, it whispered, "No, no, no..."

I slewed around, only to fall back, nearly knocking over the painting in my effort to get away from the apparition which was at that moment about to catch hold of my arm. I saw a thin and desiccated body clad only in tatters of clothing, and long-nailed hands which were more like claws reaching out to me. My eyes were drawn irresistibly upwards and with dread to its head, but to my surprise and relief there was no grinning skull. The face, with its taut skin and halo of wispy grey hair, was that of a fragile old man. Only the determined set of the mouth and the stubborn look in the pale eyes suggested that this was a revenant not to be tangled with by anyone who valued their safety and sanity.

Too startled to move, I watched as the creature turned, still whispering and muttering, and shuffled off with painful slowness down the nave. At a point level with the memorial tablet which I had examined that morning, it turned again, frowned briefly over its shoulder at me, and passed into the south aisle. I lost sight of it between the pillars, and when I got up to look down the aisle, it was empty, although again I heard the slight grating noise.

"So that was Joseph Gill," I said aloud, stating the obvious in an attempt to calm my nerves; and in the process disturbing the sparrow which recommenced its frantic fluttering. I need hardly add that I got little more work done that day.

My hopes that the ghostly visitation would prove to be an isolated occurrence were dashed the following afternoon, when I again heard the footsteps start down the church towards me. They sounded stronger and more resolute than before, and I confess that I caught no more than a brief glimpse of a grey shape before fleeing from the building in some disarray. Seizing the opportunity, the sparrow followed me out. It was clear that I would have to complete my task elsewhere, and this I did in due course by moving the Commonwealth shield to Mr Johnson's cottage, where I was not disturbed again. Not disturbed, I should say, by Joseph Gill, but Mr Johnson took such a keen interest in what I was doing, and tried so hard to help, that I did begin to wonder—ungratefully—whether being haunted might be less bothersome.

It would be impossible for restorers such as myself to consider the feelings of the dead to the same degree as those of the living when we do our work. However, when it lies within our power to please everyone I see no reason why we shouldn't try. So after finishing the repairs to the Arms, I suggested to the rector that it might be better for all concerned if the painting were donated to the Castle Museum at Colchester. After due consideration, he agreed, though I could see that he didn't understand my motives, and I had no wish to enlighten him. Between us we hatched a story to satisfy the Diocesan authorities. As I recall, we suggested that such a rare and delicate item was in danger of being destroyed by damp while it remained in the church. This the authorities accepted, and the State's Arms were hung in Colchester Castle where they have so far caused no trouble at all.

Sometimes I wonder whether Marston church was bothered by the spectre of Joseph Gill during the 1650s when the shield he so hated was in position. I could find no record of it, and I don't suppose I shall ever know. It is, anyway, of purely academic interest now that he is at rest again.

In 1977, a year after the events which I have described, I heard that a new Royal Arms had been made by a local artist for the church, in order to celebrate the Queen's Silver Jubilee. I'm sure the old Royalist was delighted!

JOAN

Here am I
Little Jumping Joan
When no one is with me
I am all alone.
(Old Nursery Rhyme)

In the Spring of 1978, my work as a restorer of ecclesiastical furnishings took me to Norton Hills, a quiet village in southern Essex, where there were still a surprising number of such places, despite their proximity to the Basildon conurbation. My task was to restore a rather beautiful late nineteenth-century reredos; a painted triptych in Pre-Raphaelite style, which was one of the treasures of St Peter's church. The rector of Norton, the Reverend Jonathan Pride, was a High

Church man—unlike his predecessor—and since he had only taken over the living a year previously, the villagers still treated him with extreme wariness. For this reason, I think, he was especially pleased to welcome me to the rectory. I was someone with whom he could relax and talk easily for the first time in months, and we hit it off from the start.

Jonathan was in his early thirties, only a few years my senior, and we found many interests in common. During the first evening of my stay, our conversation ranged over subjects too numerous to list, from the Beatles to books (at length) to Edward Burne Jones (whom I love but Jonathan confessed to finding insipid).

The topic of architecture soon come up, and prompted a guided tour of the rectory: a splendid red-brick Jacobean edifice, with highly-decorated chimneys as its most distinctive external feature; and some fine strapwork plaster moulding in several of its rooms. Although not overwhelmingly large, it boasted four bedrooms, a comfortable library-cum-study and a pretty dining room. Since the rector was single and had no living-in help, much of the space was unused, but by no means neglected. As we walked around, the approval which I expressed was never less than sincere.

Further conversation followed and we completely lost track of time, until I suddenly realised that it was getting late and I was starting to yawn. After saying our good-nights, and as I headed towards the guest bedroom, a look of concern suddenly clouded Jonathan's face. "Promise me, Jane," he said, "that if you hear any noises in the night you won't leave your room."

I must have assumed he was joking, or perhaps I was so tired that it didn't sink in fully, but whatever the reason, I'm rather surprised now that I promised so willingly and without question.

As is so often the case when one is over-tired, I simply could not get to sleep: an hour later I was still tossing and turning. Thus, when I heard pattering footsteps outside my door, in the corridor which led to the stairs, I knew at once that I was not dreaming. The steps seemed to belong to a small child who was skipping and running along in an erratic fashion. They could not be the feet of the rector, and he did not own any pets whose nocturnal wanderings could produce such sounds. "I promised I wouldn't leave my room," I thought to myself, "but I can still open the door and look out. I hope it's not rats."

Unfortunately, by the time I reached the door, the footsteps had started down the stairs, and although the corridor was well lit by the bright moon, shining in through the landing window, I saw nothing unexpected. Then a soft crying began in the hallway below me. I think I would have gone to investigate but, at that moment, Jonathan came out of his bedroom, halfway between me and the staircase.

"You heard it, did you?" he said. "I wondered if you would."

"What is it?" I asked predictably. "Shouldn't we go down and see?"

"*No!*" he almost shouted. "There's no need. I'll tell you all about it tomorrow, but please go back to sleep now. The crying will stop in a few minutes."

Feeling slightly disgruntled, I climbed back into

bed, and listened to the child-like wailing as it rose in a mournful and heart-rending crescendo before fading away to nothing, as Jonathan had assured me it would.

Next morning, I came down early, having slept well for the remaining few hours of the night. Jonathan was already eating breakfast, and as he helped me to some cereal, I waited expectantly for his explanation.

"I'm sorry I didn't prepare you for it yesterday," he began. "But I honestly hoped you wouldn't be affected. This house is haunted. Of course, you don't need me to tell you that."

I agreed, spluttering through a mouthful of cornflakes that it was not the first ghost I had encountered.

"The reason I didn't want you to see it last night—as you would have done if you'd gone downstairs—was that I saw it once myself, and it isn't something I'd wish on anyone else." He paused to butter some toast before resuming. "Ever since moving in, I've heard the ghost regularly each evening, although the timing varies—it's always an hour or two after I've gone to bed. Naturally I tried to get to the bottom of things and, if I remember rightly, it was during my second night here that I followed the noises down to the hallway.

"The culprit was standing near the front door: a tiny figure in a loose white garment of some sort. She seemed very solid, but she was—to put it bluntly—no more than a cadaver. I could see the bones of her arms through the dried-up skin, and her head was a stark white skull." Jonathan shuddered. "I'm ashamed to say that my faith failed me then. I turned tail, and spent the rest of the night cowering under the bedclothes!" An understandable reaction, I assured him.

"Afterwards, I briefly considered exorcism, but didn't feel that it would be right. Despite her appearance, she is not an evil ghost; I'm convinced of that. If she wishes to haunt my house, I must allow her to do so—she was here first, after all. She has never harmed me, and I find I'm starting to get used to her."

"I'm sure you're right," I said. "Although I don't envy you having to live with it. Why, by the way, do you call the spectre 'she'? Judging from your description it might be of either sex."

"Ah..." my friend smiled slightly. "After a good deal of effort I finally managed to extract a little information about her from one of the more garrulous villagers. Apparently, she has been known for hundreds of years, and her name, traditionally, is Joan. That aside, her identity is a mystery to the parishioners, although there are vague tales of her being the victim of a hideous murder. Some say a former rector was the killer.

"I treated these stories with a pinch of salt," he added. "But a few months ago I had a spot of luck when sorting through the parish chest: I discovered a set of Overseers' Poor Records, complete for the seventeenth century. Being keen to learn all I could about the history of my parish, I read them through... and I think I found our Joan.

"Look, why don't you come over to the church and I'll show you, before you start work this morning? There's a graffito I'd like you to see as well."

I agreed willingly and within ten minutes we were ensconced in the cramped vestry, with the Poor Records open before us. Jonathan pointed out the relevant passages, which I studied carefully. They related to one Ruth Lange and her six-year-old daughter Joan, who both received Parish Relief in 1653. The payments had ceased in October when Ruth had died by her own hand, carrying her daughter with her when she jumped into the River Crouch just outside Norton and drowned. Labourers on a nearby farm witnessed the event, but were too far away to prevent it. By the time they reached the scene, they could only pull the bodies from the water.

Because of the unusual nature of the case, the Overseers had included some useful background notes: the father of Joan Lange was a Royalist soldier who was killed while fighting in Colchester in the Civil War, when the child was hardly more than a babe in arms. Ruth Lange seems to have reacted to her early widowhood by becoming slightly deranged, but the rector took her in as an assistant housekeeper. This was in 1648. In 1653, the old rector died, and was replaced by a staunch Puritan who immediately turned the Langes out as Royalist sympathisers. It was then that they began receiving Poor Relief.

Reading between the lines I deduced that such help as they got from the Parish was begrudged by the now largely Puritan villagers, who were not too sorry to see them go. (Ironically, those same villagers were eager enough to pledge allegiance to Charles II at his Restoration seven years later. A large Royal Coat of Arms still in the church is dated

'1660' and festooned with such loyal inscriptions as, 'Fear God, Honour the King, and Meddle Not With Them That Are Given To Change.') When I had finished, Jonathan moved the Overseers' Records to one side and opened up the Parish Registers for the relevant period. Under the deaths listed for 1653 were Joan and Ruth Lange, with a brief note in the margin to the effect that Ruth, being a suicide and a murderess, was buried outside the churchyard in unconsecrated ground, while little Joan was placed in an unmarked pauper's grave somewhere near the church.

"A tragic story," I commented finally. "The poor woman must have been quite desperate. And I can only think that little Joan haunts the Rectory because it was the Puritan rector who contributed so greatly to the tragedy. Not that there weren't similar or worse cases of heartlessness among those loyal to the Crown... What about the graffito you mentioned? Is it connected in some way?"

"Oh yes," said my friend, getting up and putting the records away. "I nearly forgot about it, but it really is very intriguing and quite relevant."

I followed him out into the body of the church, where he knelt down and pointed to a spot hidden behind the pulpit. Some words were crudely incised into the plaster of the wall, and with difficulty I made them out:

Joan Lange
All Alone
God Forgyve Me
T. Cotter

I looked at Jonathan for elucidation. "Thomas Cotter was the name of the Puritan rector," he said. "It seems that he came to regret his actions."

* * *

That night I did not expect to sleep well, at least not until Joan Lange had completed her rounds; but I dropped off very quickly, and slept soundly. Just before waking I had a short vivid dream: I was standing in St Peter's churchyard, by the high stone wall which separated it from the rectory garden. In front of me was an enchanting little girl; even though her face was puffy and stained with tears she was still one of the prettiest creatures I have ever seen. She was jumping up repeatedly and trying to reach for someone or something on the other side of the wall, but each time she fell back, crying sadly to herself.

I heard a small voice saying, "Please try again; I will help you", and then, suddenly, I realised that I could see, or at least sense, what was behind the wall. It was a young woman, so haggard and worn that she was painful to look at. Her hysterical attempts to get a grip and clamber over the barrier were being continuously frustrated by what appeared to be slime or mud on her hands, making them slide over the stones and leaving rows of greenish-brown marks. This was all I saw before the vision ended.

My first thought on waking was: "We must pull down the wall". It was two or three minutes before I remembered that only a low privet hedge now separated the churchyard from the rectory garden.

As I expected, Jonathan was sympathetic when told about my dream. "Perhaps we can bring the poor little soul and her mother back together again," he remarked. "It's strictly unorthodox, and I would have to make sure that the archdeacon didn't get to know about it, but I'd be quite willing to re-inter Ruth Lange's bones in consecrated ground if only we could find them."

"We could at least try," I said. "And I believe we ought to start searching at the spot where I saw the figure of the woman in my dream."

It was just after one o'clock on the following morning that we ventured forth with our spades, thankful that the rectory garden was not overlooked, and that heavy clouds covered the moon.

The bones were exactly where we had hoped to find them, although it required several hours of hard work to reach down to them and remove them all from the earth. We took the remains to a secluded area of the churchyard, where we made a small grave for them, and Jonathan said a few words of blessing. I was touched by the impromptu ceremony, although, at any moment I expected to be set upon by irate villagers and accused of bodysnatching or desecration. Fortunately nothing of that sort occurred, and to our joy the rectory ghost did not return in the ensuing days. It seems that we had accomplished what Joan Lange had been wanting for over three hundred years; to be reunited with the mother she still loved in spite of everything.

After some of the initial relief and pleasure had worn off, our single remaining worry was that someone would find out about our scandalous behaviour. We had disguised the disturbed ground as best we could, but when the old fellow who helped to tend the garden arrived a few days later, he soon noticed the change.

"Been busy gardening then, Parson?" he said.

Turning an embarrassed pink, Jonathan managed to stammer out a reply: "Er... well... yes. Actually I was making a start on building a rockery. I thought it would look nice down there by the hedge."

The old man took him at his word, and insisted on taking charge of the proceedings. When I revisited the village recently to have an informal dinner with my clerical friend, I'm pleased to say that the rockery was ablaze with colour in the summer sun, and a credit to all concerned.

ANNIE'S GHOST

The four of us were sitting around in various stages of exhaustion, gazing with horror at the half-unpacked tea-chests on all sides, and wondering which one contained the teapot. My aunt and uncle, along with my teenage cousin Annie, were moving from their house in Chelmsford into a comfortable cottage at Infield, near Brentwood; and in a moment of weakness I had offered to help.

The move had been accompanied by its inevitable quota of traumas, not the least being the discovery, when we arrived, that the electricity had not been reconnected. After a number of phone calls it was finally sorted out—hence our search for the teapot—but it had, in the meantime, delayed the unpacking somewhat. By five o'clock there was still a great deal to do, but we were all too worn out to tackle it.

"Today has really gone fast," I said, stirring slightly to stretch my aching legs. "It's getting dark already and we still haven't got any curtains up." Everyone turned to look out of the French windows into the garden, which was beginning to lose its colour in the gathering dusk. Suddenly Annie gasped.

"Did you see that?"

"What?" we all said together. None of us had noticed anything out of the ordinary.

"You are an unobservant lot." She shook her head in disgust. "Down by the bottom fence there was a figure—a funny old man, all thin and yellowish. Ugh! he was horrible! It didn't look as though he was wearing any clothes either, just rags. He ran off into the bushes when he saw us looking out."

"I must say you've moved into a nice area," I joked. "It seems to come equipped with a resident streaker!"

Of course we laughed the whole thing off. If Annie had seen someone, we agreed, it must have been a rather ancient jogger in the playing fields at the end of the garden. Next day, I returned to my own home, and thought no more about it. But two weeks later, when I phoned to see how the unpacking was progressing (and to ask whether they'd finally found the teapot), I was surprised to hear that the mystery man had become quite a nuisance.

"We've got used to you telling us about the spooks you see all over the place," my aunt said, "but we were hoping that it hadn't rubbed off on

Annie. No such luck. That strange figure she saw when we first moved in has been reappearing every night. Sometimes he creeps up quite close to the cottage, and it's got Annie so scared that she spends ages each evening double-checking the locks on all the doors. The ridiculous thing is that your uncle and I can't see him. We did think that Annie might be making it up, but it isn't like her to play silly games. Seriously, we're a bit worried—there's definitely something peculiar going on, and Annie's health is starting to suffer. You don't have any ideas, do you?"

Luckily I was within a few days of finishing my current church restoration job and I arranged to go down to Infield as soon as possible. If nothing else, perhaps I would see the creature (another to add to my list!), and thus be able to reassure my cousin that she was not imagining it.

When I arrived at my relatives' new home I noticed that the whole family looked drawn; Annie was noticeably pale, and not her usual ebullient self at all. As the sun began to set, she became even quieter. I managed to persuade her to help me with the washing-up—leaving her parents to relax—and, on our own in the kitchen, I encouraged her to tell me what she had seen.

"Every night he turns up," she said. "It's usually around this time, although he hasn't appeared yet tonight. I've had several good sights of him now, but one was more than enough. He's all bony and his skin looks like paper; it's drawn back from his mouth so that he's grinning almost like a skeleton. I don't think he's alive. He's got hair down to his waist and a beard that's even longer. There's a bit of cloth draped around him, but it doesn't cover up much."

The kitchen window faced the same way as the French doors in the living room, and as my cousin was speaking I found that my eyes were being drawn to the garden, but there was no sign of the old man. The evening was still and peaceful, disturbed only by an occasional squawk, which Annie explained was from a pet tawny owl in its pen next door.

It was when she returned from a trip to the larder, having unloaded a precariously-balanced pile of plates, that she suddenly exclaimed: "There he is now—you must be able to see him; he's just by the goldfish pond".

I could see nothing, although I confess that when Annie described how the spook was hurrying towards us with arms raised threateningly, I joined her in backing away into the hall.

"So he's invisible to you as well," she said sadly. "Perhaps I am going crazy after all. Why else would I be the only one to see him?"

Later, after Annie had disappeared to her room to watch television on her portable set, I asked her parents whether the previous owners of the cottage had reported anything odd about the place.

"When you're selling a house," my uncle replied, "you don't advertise that sort of thing, do you? But the Pearsons lived here for twenty years, and they were its first owners; when they left it was to retire to Cornwall, so I don't think they can have had any trouble."

An idea occurred to me. "Did they have any children, do you know?" I asked.

"No, they were both career people, I believe."

"And am I right in guessing that Annie hasn't had any young friends staying here in the evening yet?"

My uncle nodded.

"That might be the answer then," I said. "The old ghost only appears to children or teenagers... But if that's so, there must surely be a reason why he acts in this way. I think I'll go along to the Essex Record Office tomorrow and see if I can track down anything about him."

My aunt looked thoughtful. "We did wonder whether the cottage could be on an old site; this whole row of houses was built in what used to be the grounds of Infield Manor, but the Manor itself was right over on the other side of the playing fields, so I don't see how that can have any connection."

"Well, I'll find out what I can," I said. "Though I'm afraid the odds are against me solving the mystery."

As it turned out, I discovered the occupation in life of the ugly spectre within fifteen minutes of my arrival at the Record Office. Consulting the large-scale Ordnance Survey map of the area, which was published in 1863, I quickly noted that the location of my relatives' house coincided almost exactly with a plot in the grounds of Infield Manor where a hermitage was marked. Numerous temples and grottoes were dotted around nearby, so evidently the hermitage was an eighteenth-century folly and not an ancient site. Rich Georgian landowners often employed old men to live as hermits or anchorites in picturesque little buildings. They were quite fashionable garden ornaments at one time—probably the higher-class equivalent of our plastic gnomes. "Annie's ghost must have been one of those poor fellows," I thought.

However this didn't answer the question of why the spook existed, and why he seemed to be seen only by children. After checking through a few of the published sources of information about the Manor, and gaining nothing of relevance for my pains, I was beginning to resign myself to the likelihood that the identity of the hermit was lost in the mists of time. Then, as I was on the point of leaving, one of the archivists came up to my desk carrying a heavy, leather-bound book in her hands.

"Excuse me," she whispered. "I notice that you're doing research on Infield Manor. Would this album be of any interest to you? It's a collection of pictures and anecdotes about the Manor, which a lady in Brentwood recently bequeathed to us—we haven't had time to include it in our index yet. I believe an ancestor of hers wrote and drew the contents in the 1850s."

I accepted the book with thanks but with no great hope of finding any clues within it. However, I was wrong. After a few pages devoted to sketches of the house and grounds, all nicely laid out and annotated in a clear, legible longhand, undoubtedly feminine, I came across an illustration of the hermitage as it was in 1850. Despite its ruinous state I could tell that it had once been a very pretty, Gothic-style building. As I read the accompanying notes I saw that I had found my answers. Following a short description of the tiny cell, which explained that it was erected in 1780 by the squire on a whim of his wife's, the writer went on:

The Lady insisted that a real anchorite be hired to live in the folly; and an elderly man, one Richard Bankes, was chosen for the position. At the time, my father was working as a stable-lad at the Big House, and he has told me that Mr Bankes was a disagreeable sort of gentleman. Rumours about him were rife, the most tenacious being that he was a person of great wealth and had hidden a hoard of treasure in or near the hermitage. All the lads, together with some of the younger maids employed at the Manor, took to taunting him and trying to get him to reveal the location of his riches, but the recluse would say nothing. Eventually he died, and the secret of his money—if there was any—died with him.

Although the old man's life had reached its natural span, my father and the other youths felt that their actions had in some way contributed to his death. Superstitiously, they would not go near the hermit's cell to look for the treasure; and since, in the meantime, the Lady had become bored with anchorites, the building was neglected and fast fell into ruin. Even now, over seventy years later, none of the village children will play near the remains of the little folly, for stories are told of peculiar figures seen in the vicinity.

I copied out these paragraphs before taking the album back to the archivist, thanking her profusely for her assistance.

On returning to Infield I showed my transcription to the family, who were thrilled with it; Annie in particular.

"So it looks as though Richard Bankes haunts only teenagers, because they were the people who made his last years so unhappy," I explained. "I'd guess, from the fact that he continues to be a nuisance, that there really was some sort of treasure, and probably it's still buried deep under the garden here. Unless you want to dig holes all over the place though, I don't think you're going to find it. If it had been fairly close to the surface I'm sure someone would already have discovered it while gardening. Still, you might consider buying a metal detector, just in case..."

"But what should we do about the old horror?" asked my aunt. "I don't much fancy living with him, even if Annie is the only one who can see him. She's not a nervous child, but it's bound to have an effect on her, and her O-levels are coming up in two years."

After a good deal of thought, all I could suggest was that they could see a priest about some sort of exorcism, but I didn't hold out much hope of its success. Several minutes later we looked up from our discussion and noticed that Annie was missing.

"Where's the girl got to now?" my uncle frowned. "Here we are worrying about her, and she's probably gone off to watch television again."

Then we heard the back door slam and my cousin came in, beaming broadly. "It's all right, you needn't worry any more. I've just been out into the garden getting rid of the ghost..."

She ignored our incredulous expressions and continued. "I went out and reasoned with him. The horrid creature didn't show himself, but I knew he was there—though if any neighbours saw me they must have thought I was an idiot, standing on the lawn talking to thin air! I said I was really sorry that some young people had bothered him, but we weren't all so bad. As far as I was concerned he could keep his stupid money and needn't worry about my stealing it. If he would just go away and not disturb me, then I would leave him and his treasure alone. When I'd finished, he'd gone—he really had; I could tell! I don't think he was so bad after all."

As Annie hurried into her bedroom to watch her favourite TV show, we looked at each other and burst out laughing: it was an unorthodox solution but maybe it deserved to succeed. Personally I doubted whether it had. These situations are rarely so easily resolved, but then again the supernatural doesn't often comes into contact with someone as determined as Annie. All we could do was to wait and see.

These events occurred six months ago, and nothing has been seen of Mr Richard Bankes since, so Annie's technique might just have worked. The household is now back to normal, and the three of them have completely settled into their new home. They haven't bought a metal detector though, and much to the puzzlement of friends and relatives, they have decided to name their cottage "The Hermitage"!

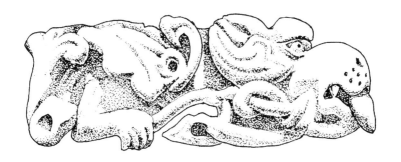

MARGARET AND CATHERINE

25th July 1980
7 The Grove
Crossley
Essex

Dear Jane,
I remember that when you visited us last Spring, you were intrigued by the Bisham monument in Crossley Abbey. At the moment I am helping to compile an inventory of the books and manuscripts in the library at Crossley Hall, which (as you may know) was the home of the Bishams until they died out in the seventeenth century. One

document seems to throw some light on the unusual aspect of the monument which you noticed. I enclose a photocopy that I hope will interest you.

    When are you coming down this way again?

Best Wishes,
Ralph Bradshawe

PS: We seem to be in the news here at present. One of the local children is missing, poor mite, and I hear the river which runs through the grounds of the Hall is to be dragged tomorrow.

As soon as I read the letter from my cousin, I recalled the memorial mentioned. It's a large, Tudor tomb with reclining life-size figures of a lady and gentleman, situated in the north aisle of the Abbey: a building which—since the Dissolution of the Monasteries—had been the parish church of the Essex village of Crossley, now little more than a suburb of north London. The monument had puzzled me because the carved panel along the front, depicting a row of praying offspring, was rather out of the ordinary. Of the five daughters shown, three were kneeling modestly in their Elizabethan caps and ruffs, but the fourth had half-turned to look at the fifth and smallest, who was tugging at her sleeve and obviously trying to draw her away from her devotions.

    I had remarked to Ralph that there must surely be some sort of story behind the figures, and evidently he'd remembered this. When I unfolded the copy of the manuscript, however, I revised my appreciation of his thoughtfulness. The text, in tiny, neat writing on two large sheets of paper, was in Latin. "I suppose I shall have to translate this," I said to myself. "He could at least have included his own reading of it."

Before putting the document away to deal with later, the name of the writer, at the top of the first page, caught my eye: Elizabeth Bisham. I was fairly certain that I had seen the name before, presumably on the tomb. Some ten minutes later, having checked through several notebooks in search of the transcript I had made of the memorial inscription at Crossley, I found that my suspicions were correct.

Apparently the Bisham monument commemorated Sir Henry Bisham (1539-1592) and his wife, Joan (1547-1576). The inscription painted a fulsomely rosy picture of Sir Henry, his influential position, and the faultless way in which he fulfilled his responsibilities as husband and father; the later particularly after the death of his wife at the birth of their fifth child. Joan Bisham was also portrayed as a paragon of virtue, although she merited just one line of text.

At the bottom was an addition in a later hand: And also their daughters, Elizabeth (1570-1630), Mary (1571-1600) and Alice (1573-1613)

"At that rate of production," I thought, "it's hardly surprising the poor mother didn't survive her fifth. But I wonder why the other two daughters weren't buried with the rest?"

* * *

It was not until a couple of days later that I had an evening free to tackle the manuscript. An exact translation would be tedious to read so I shan't trouble you with it: instead a summary will suffice.

The document was dated 1627, when Elizabeth Bisham would have been fifty-seven. In a short preamble she gave her reasons for writing the account: it was, she said, in order to explain how she came to be the last of her line, and why such a prosperous and large family should have produced no heirs.

After this, there was a list of the family members. The daughters not mentioned on the tomb were, I discovered, the two youngest: Catherine, who was born in 1574, and Margaret, born in 1576. Kate, it appeared, was the apple of her father's eye, but for Margaret he held a scarcely-veiled dislike, due to the fact that his wife had died while giving birth to her. Thus Sir Henry felt that Margaret had robbed him of the possibility of producing a male heir. He could have married again, of course, but according to Elizabeth it was out of the question: after Lady Bisham's death, he grew more and more morose, and not only lost most of his friends, but also his important position at Court.

Although the other daughters were extremely fond of their youngest sibling perhaps in order to compensate for her father's lack of love, she became increasingly bitter and uncontrollable. Elizabeth who, as the eldest had taken on the role of mother to the family, spent most of her time trying to keep the peace between father and offspring. In this manner life continued until June

1590, when Sir Henry was pleased to announce the betrothal of his second daughter, Mary, to a very suitable young man. The wedding was planned for eighteenth months hence, but several things happened in the intervening time which tragically succeeded in preventing it.

A few weeks after the betrothal, a band of gypsies arrived in Crossley and settled temporarily in a nearby wood. The rebellious Margaret was attracted to them, and became quite friendly with a handsome, dark-haired boy who was just a little older than her fourteen years. When her father heard of this he flew into a rage and forbade her to leave the house until the travellers moved on. Sometime that day, Margaret disappeared. Sir Henry told the rest of the family that she had run out after their argument, and he'd been unable to stop her. When she did not return, a search for the gypsies was made, but they were gone, and it was presumed that they had taken the wayward girl with them.

From that day on (the text continued), bad luck seemed to pursue the Bishams. The three older daughters all contracted smallpox and were hideously scarred. So severe was the damage that there was no question of Mary's marriage taking place; and Elizabeth herself was so badly affected that she had to walk with the aid of a stick for the rest of her life. The only one to avoid the outbreak was Catherine who thereafter became even more favoured by her father.

Nearly two years after Margaret's disappearance, the family was busily preparing for another wedding: this time Catherine was the bride-to-be, but instead of being thrilled and excited at the prospect, she seemed to be preoccupied with something else. Finally Elizabeth drew from her sister the confession that she thought she had seen Margaret several times in the garden at night, beckoning and trying to get Kate to go out to her. Enquiries were made in the village but no gypsies had been in the area for some time, so Elizabeth, in her solid no-nonsense way, decided that Catherine was suffering from nothing worse than nerves because of her forthcoming marriage. Sir Henry's reaction, when told of his favourite daughter's experience, was rather different: he went suddenly pale and refused to speak of it.

One midsummer day, Kate said resignedly to her sisters: "I feel that I must go away with Margaret"; and that evening, despite their attempts to convince her of the foolishness of such action, and their constant assurances that there were no gypsies nearby, she was gone, leaving no trace. In the course of the next four weeks, Sir Henry's health declined so rapidly that the remaining daughters, immersed in the search for Catherine, hardly realised what was happening, until they were all summoned to his death bed. (At this point the manuscript became very difficult to read, presumably reflecting the writer's emotional state.) The old man lying there, dwarfed by the four-poster bed, was a feeble, shrunken shadow of the father they knew, and it was several minutes before they saw that he was trying to speak. Elizabeth could hear nothing until she leaned very close and held her ear to his lips. It was then that Sir Henry confessed to her: he had strangled young Margaret in a fit of rage when she threatened to run off with the gypsies. The body, he said, had been hidden in his room until nightfall and then thrown in the river.

Elizabeth's unanswerable query was, "But if Margaret was dead, who could have taken Kate from us?"

The last paragraph of the text was devoted to a brief and depressing description of the lives of the surviving sisters. None of them married, and neither Mary nor Alice lived beyond the age of forty. They both died in ignorance of their father's terrible deed. In 1627 Elizabeth had been alone at the Hall for fourteen years. Her final plea was heart-rending: "How much longer must I endure this loneliness?" Remembering that the monumental inscription gave her date of death as 1630, I was happy to think that her cry for release was soon to be answered.

This, then, was the gist of the story which unfolded as I translated the document. My progress was slow and involved much resorting to a Latin dictionary and grammar so, despite the dramatic nature of the narrative, I found my eyelids drooping as I reached the end. Suddenly I jerked awake from a doze, or thought I did. Looking around I noticed, with a sort of dull surprise, that the top page of the manuscript had changed. The writing was still visible, but now it was overlaid, almost like a palimpsest, with a moving scene. Although there was a slight mistiness, I could make out a large house, red-bricked in the popular Tudor style. In front was a terrace, and steps leading down to a garden, pleasantly laid out with shrubs and flowers. As I watched, two pale figures ran along the terrace and started down the steps. One was a young woman, clad in a white nightgown and with long chestnut hair flowing to her waist. She was skipping alongside the second figure which I saw altogether less clearly. For that I'm quite grateful. The greyish ankle-length garment covering most of its body must once have been a very pretty dress, until it began to rot. And I could see enough of the blotchy, cadaverous head, and the bony claw with which it clutched the plump hand of its companion, to know that it was not alive. Not, at least, in any normal sense of the word.

Obviously the creature had somehow hidden its true appearance from the young woman. Indeed, she was laughing and giggling as she chattered with it, as though they were the best of friends. What shocked me was that the dead thing seemed to be replying in a like manner.

I cried out to warn the girl, but of course she could not hear me. Then I must have fainted, because I felt myself falling forward, and I think I hit my head on the desk. When I came to, the manuscript had returned to normal and, on checking my watch. I found that only two or three minutes had passed since the completion of my translation.

Even now I still don't know whether I was dreaming or not, but the truth of my vision did receive some confirmation a couple of days later when another letter arrived from my cousin, enclosing a clipping from the previous week's edition of the local newspaper. The letter simply said: "I thought this news item might appeal to you as an amazing coincidence in relation to the Bisham document which I sent several days ago. I'm sure you will see the connection".

The cutting reported that divers, searching the river at Crossley for the missing child mentioned by Ralph in his earlier letter, had discovered two skeletons, half buried in the mud of the riverbed. "Expert opinion" was that the remains were of two females, who had both been under the age of twenty-five when they died, at least three hundred years ago.

The missing child has still not been found.

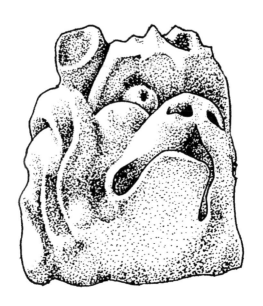

NE RESURGAT

"There is a very strange story attached to that memorial tablet, Miss Bradshawe," said the rector, pointing to a simple stone slab on the north wall of his little church. St Mary's, Northbridge, is a square red-brick Georgian building balanced atmospherically on the edge of the mud-flats of the River Crouch estuary in eastern Essex; and I was there to clean a rather grand wall monument to some early nineteenth-century members of the local Barkstone family (a bequest having been made for the purpose by a recent descendant).

The much humbler memorial to which the Reverend Jim Shaw and myself were addressing our attention at the moment, however, was immediately to the right of the other. The inscription was terse, to say the least:

HANNAH WAITE
1809-1851
Ne Resurgat

"Have you ever seen such a motto before?" the rector asked, in a tone which made it clear that he was certain I had not.

"No, I can't say I have," I replied. "*Resurgam* means 'I will rise again'—it's found quite often on funeral hatchments—but *Ne Resurgat* looks like a subjunctive so I suppose it must mean 'Let her not rise again'. I can only think that someone wanted to make sure Hannah Waite stayed where she was!"

"You've hit the nail on the head," he nodded. "I went into the history of the Waites ten years ago when I took up the incumbency here, and I always meant to write it up for a local magazine, but never had the time. It caused quite a stir when it happened. Apparently Ernest and Hannah Waite lived in a cottage which used to stand a few hundred yards from here. Ernest was a violent man and a drunkard, but his wife seemed able to cope with him until he somehow got the idea that she was a witch who was torturing him with terrible pains in the head."

I smiled and was about to make some comment, but the Reverend Shaw forestalled me, "Yes, you're right of course—the liquor was almost certainly the culprit, and his long-suffering wife completely innocent. At any rate, one day Mrs Waite disappeared. Many of the neighbours believed that her husband had done away with her, but there was no proof. A week or two later Ernest also vanished, and when some of the villagers broke into the cottage to look for the couple, no trace of them could be found. Not, that is, until one of the searchers opened the larder door to reveal a grisly discovery: the decomposing head of Hannah Waite. That object was eventually interred here in the church; and the husband was never seen again, so I imagine he must have panicked and run away, maybe to Harwich and a ship abroad."

"There was a superstition that the only way to prevent a witch or vampire from returning after death was decapitation," I said, after the rector had finished. "Perhaps that's why Ernest Waite removed his wife's head. I must say that it's certainly a very nasty story—I'm not sure I should thank you for telling it to me."

"Well," he chuckled, "it could have been worse, Miss... er, Jane—I could have waited a few minutes and told you over lunch!"

Grateful for small mercies I followed him to the rectory for the promised meal, stopping briefly on the way while he pointed out the site of the Waites' cottage.

In the afternoon I had cause to remember Jim Shaw's narrative. I use a small step-ladder for work which is just too high to reach from the ground; and I needed it for the Barkstone monument. Stepping down after finishing the day's labours, I missed my footing on the bottom rung and made a grab for the wall to steady myself. The plaster gave way under my hand, and I was precipitated to the ground with a bump, in a shower of plaster dust.

For a few seconds my only thought was to make sure that no bones were broken, and no damage done—to me at least—but after reassuring myself of this, the realisation suddenly dawned that my hand, as it went through the wall, had come into contact with something peculiar; something which had felt distinctly like a set of teeth. This was, I'm relieved to say, rather more like what Nigel Pargeter found under Walter Gabriel's bath in *The Archers* than the "mouth, with teeth, and with hair about it", which poor Dunning encountered under his pillow in Dr James' *'Casting the Runes'*. Peering into the hole in the wall, I came face to face with a dry, lifeless skull, which I quickly deduced to be the paltry remains of Hannah Waite, whose memorial was a few feet above. In my fall I had knocked the top of the skull away from the jaw-bone, and also dislodged a small, tarnished metal crucifix which now lay to one side.

Brushing myself down I went to tell the rector of my discovery. I was naturally more than a little unsure of what his reaction would be to the havoc I had caused in the church, but I need not have worried. He was in his element, and spent the entire evening telephoning the local newspapers to make arrangements for reporters and photographers to call the next day. I was left to my own devices, so I made some cheese sandwiches for my supper, and went to my bedroom with a paperback thriller. Before getting into bed, I spent a few moments at the window, gazing out at the grey expanse of the mud-flats spread before me and lit by the full moon which glittered strangely on the many little pools. "What an ideal location for a ghost story," I thought.

Whether the view from the window disturbed me more than I realised, or whether it was just the sandwiches, I had a very restless night with several unpleasant nightmares. In one of the most memorable, I seemed to be watching a scene taking place in a small, cluttered room, where a tiny, plump woman was cooking what looked like a stew, on a spotless range. Suddenly the door burst open and a burly red-faced man lurched in and, judging from his facial expression (I could hear nothing), began screaming at the woman. She gave as good as she got, but this only enraged him further, until at last he grabbed at her and, picking up a skewer from the table, started stabbing her repeatedly with it. In a dream you cannot close your eyes so I was forced to continue watching, and eventually it became clear that the man (Ernest Waite, as I had assumed by now) was not trying to inflict a mortal wound, but rather a number of superficial ones. "Why," I thought, "the drunken fool is pricking his wife to find the witch mark." Apparently he was not finding what he wanted, as each wound bled profusely. Then Hannah, who was by this time a sorry sight, abruptly clutched at her chest and fell to the floor.

My dream faded, returning almost immediately to the same location—in time to reveal Ernest Waite sawing his wife's head from her body. Mercifully my view was brief, and quickly melted into a new scene; the mud-flats outside the Waites' cottage, where Ernest was digging a hole for a wrapped bundle which lay on the ground beside him. Had it twitched slightly? I fervently hoped not.

I think I awoke at this point. I vaguely remember sitting up and looking at my travelling clock on the bedside table, but not taking in the time. Sleep soon returned, and it seemed that I was dreaming again at once (although, in fact my final dream of the night must have come some hours later). I was back on the mud-flats, observing a running figure which approached with some rapidity. It was Ernest Waite, fleeing towards the river as if the Devil himself was at his heels. As he passed the spot where my dream-self stood, I realised that a second figure was following in pursuit. At first it looked like an unbelievably gigantic toad, but when it got closer I saw that it was a headless, human form. The body was heavily caked with mud, which dripped from the tatters of cloth hanging from its frame. Its arms were stretched stiffly out, reaching towards the prey upon which it was gaining fast.

If I'd had time to think, I suppose I would have wondered at the purposeful and deliberate way the creature ran. Without its head, it should, perhaps, have been groping and hesitant, but on the contrary it seemed to know exactly where it was going and what it intended to do.

It quickly drew abreast of me, and I cowered back—not wishing to transfer its attentions to me—but as it continued on its relentless course, my terror suddenly left me, and I was overcome by a wave of compassion and empathy for this poor being who had once been a woman. At that moment my dream-self was drawn irresistibly *into* the body of Hannah Waite. I shared her insane, overpowering hatred for the man who had killed her and buried her where she could have no rest;

and I shared the awareness of her pitiful remnant of a body—the rankness and the pain. I was blind, but although surrounded by darkness I saw quite clearly the figure of Ernest Waite, only a few yards ahead of me now, and struggling to free his sinking legs from the marshy ground.

As Hannah reached her panic-stricken husband I was flooded with a feeling of triumph. I wanted to stay, to enjoy and be a part of her revenge, but I felt myself being pulled away again, and my head was filled with a drumming noise.

I awoke to the sound of the rector, hammering on my door. It was ten o'clock, I had overslept, and the house was in uproar: during the night, it seemed, someone had got into the church and stolen the skull from its recess. Reverend Shaw was full of self-recriminations because, in the excitement of the previous evening, he had left the church door unlocked. A careful search of the building and the churchyard by a small group of us, led by the local constable, produced no clues. The constable was puzzled by the fact that the thief had taken the skull, which possessed no monetary value whatsoever, but had left the altar candlesticks and other small items worth several hundred pounds. I must say that I was not puzzled at all.

I wish I could tell you that I found a trail of muddy footprints leading to and from the hole in the wall, but I'm afraid this account has no such satisfactory conclusion. However, no living thief was ever found, and the skull was not recovered. These facts, combined with the untroubled sleep which I enjoyed during the rest of my stay in the village, lead me to believe that Hannah Waite now rests complete and peaceful in her marshy grave.

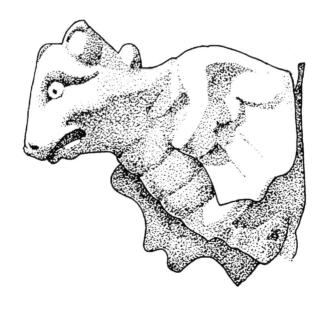

THE BLUE BOAR OF TOTENHOE

When new acquaintances discover that I restore woodcarvings and paintwork—mostly in old churches—for a living, they often ask me one of two questions. The first is "Ooh, spooky—have you ever seen a ghost?". In that case I'm very tempted to bore them for hours with my experiences. The second is along the lines of "Will you have a look at our valuable family heirloom?", in which case they're the ones who can bore *me* for hours (I've been known to consider sending them a bill for my professional services afterwards!). Usually the objects which I'm shown on these occasions are of little interest and no great worth. I once tried, and failed, to convince a determined 'expert' that his rather nice wooden goblet was not the Holy Grail and had probably been bought in Woolworths in the 1950s.

But now and then I come across something out of the ordinary. Just such a case was the strange painting which I examined in the attic of the Blue Boar Inn; a small Victorian building close to the medieval church of All Saints, Totenhoe, a few miles south of Colchester. I was lodging at the Inn while I restored the carvings on a Jacobean pulpit in the church: since the rectory was being redecorated at the time, it had not been possible for me to stay there.

Mrs Miles, the landlady of the Blue Boar, was an amiable middle-aged widow; very business-like, but still willing to spend time chatting with a guest. One morning, soon after my arrival, we were talking about this and that as she served me with a tasty breakfast of creamy scrambled eggs and piping hot toast.

"I know you're busy," she said hesitantly, "but if you've got a few minutes to spare before you go over to the church today, I have a painted panel which I'd very much like you to see. I think it could be an old inn sign, and I'd love to know whether it's antique or not. It must be much more than twenty years old anyway—my husband and I found it, hidden away and already in a filthy state, when we first moved here in 1958. Unfortunately the surface is so very dirty that I can't make out what it's meant to depict. There's a large shape in the centre which looks as though it might be a blue boar, but except for running a duster over it I've never dared to try cleaning it to find out—with my luck I would take all the paint off with the dirt!"

Inn signs can be fascinating curiosities. I've always been interested in them, and not just because many of the artists—sometimes itinerants, sometimes locals—were also responsible for work of one sort or another in churches. So when I told Mrs Miles that I would be glad to see the picture, I actually meant it.

The attic which we entered shortly afterwards was filled to overflowing with the sorts of things that people refuse to throw away "because they might come in useful one day". We picked our way carefully between dusty cardboard boxes, a pram with no wheels, a moth-eaten teddy-bear, and what looked like the remains of a couple of old lawn mowers, before reaching the far end where a large, dark board was lying propped against the wall. The harsh illumination from the unshaded light bulb revealed a good solid panel of oak, in a narrow frame; but no details of the painting could be seen except for a vague shape in the centre.

"Yes, this is definitely an inn sign," I said. "The holes in the top of the frame were probably intended to take a hanging bracket." After a brief examination, I added, "But I'm afraid it isn't very old—no more than fifty years, I'd say. The funny thing is that it shows no sign of weathering. I don't think it was ever hung outside, or not for long anyway."

I could see that the innkeeper was a little disappointed, but she cheered up when I suggested I might have a go at cleaning the painting in the evenings, after I'd finished work in the church. "The dirt is only superficial," I said. "I could have it almost as good as new in a few days—you might even want to hang it up somewhere downstairs."

So it was that, after supper that night, I settled down in front of the panel, surrounded by piles of rags and cotton wool, and equipped with a bottle of solvent. Cleaning of this sort is not difficult, but if attempted by a well-meaning amateur it can result in complete disaster and sometimes the loss of a valuable work of art. I was very pleased that Mrs Miles had been sensible enough to leave well enough alone in this case.

The picture which began to be revealed over the following three evenings was undoubtedly the creation of a skilled craftsman. The subject was indeed a blue boar, but unlike the normal heraldic portrayal of this animal—seen for instance on the new sign outside Mrs Miles' hostelry—the creature here was painted in a vigorously realistic way. It was set against a naturalistic background which I quickly recognised as the main street of Totenhoe itself: on the right I could see the lych-gate at the churchyard entrance, and just beyond was the Inn. The boar was rampaging down the deserted road, and facing outwards, so that—as I removed the layers of grime and the figure became clearer—I almost felt that it might leap out at me. By comparison with its background it was a good deal larger than life-size, and its mouth was filled with a set of dreadful-looking teeth: grotesquely huge, pointed and stained with rusty red. "Not the sort of beast I'd want to meet on a dark night!" I thought.

When I showed the results of my work so far to my host, she agreed with me that the artist must have had a vivid imagination. "I'd better not hang the sign up where people can see it," she said. "I don't want to give my customers nightmares."

The next day I returned to the attic to clear away the final areas of dust from the painting, but when I pulled off the old sheet with which I had covered it, I recoiled, astonished at what I saw. The boar had moved! It seemed to be much larger and closer to the front of the scene. Its limbs and lower body had disappeared completely below the level of the bottom edge of the frame, and its revolting head, with jaws open wide in a bellow of rage, was blotting out much of the street in the background. Even more disturbingly, I thought I detected a spark of human malice in its evil little eyes.

Needless to say I did not stop to do any work. Instead I called down to Mrs Miles so that she too could see the peculiar transformation. At first sight of the panel she gave a dismayed gasp and exclaimed, "Goodness me, what on earth has happened to it? Have you been repainting it?" I pointed out that I could hardly have repainted the whole representation so brilliantly in the twenty-four hours since she had seen it last. "Then what *is* going on?" she said.

"I wish I knew," I replied. "But one thing I'm sure about is that the picture should have been left untouched. I'm definitely not going to finish cleaning it. To be honest, I would be scared that my hand might go into that ghastly mouth and be ripped off. If I were you I would consider chopping the board up for firewood."

It was with quite understandable eagerness that the innkeeper agreed. We covered the panel up again in the old sheet and then, after closing time, we manoeuvred it downstairs, struggling with it out into the backyard. I think we both got great satisfaction from breaking it up, especially since, when we removed the sheet, the blue boar seemed to have progressed a little further up the street. The wood was brittle and dry, so it burned easily enough, and no strange manifestations accompanied its destruction.

The following evening I got back to the Inn slightly later than usual, having had tea with the rector in the one room of the rectory which was not filled with builders' ladders and the smell of wet plaster. I had been puzzling all day over the phenomenon I'd witnessed, and I was pleased to find that the reverend gentleman was a very good listener. Unfortunately he had only been the incumbent for fifteen years, so he knew nothing of the circumstances surrounding the panel's creation, and was unable to explain the events which I described. Even so, I enjoyed our conversation, and returned to the Blue Boar in a cheerful mood.

As I walked into the crowded bar, intending to go straight up to my bedroom to change, Mrs Miles paused from her duties behind the pumps to call me over.

"I've been talking to Chris Gotobed here," she said, indicating a slight, pipe-smoking figure sitting nearby. "And it looks as though he has some sort of solution to our mystery. You remember the sign-painter, don't you, Chris?"

The old fellow must have been eighty at least, but he was spry and sharp as a youngster. Although a little taciturn to start with, he became quite voluble when I offered to refill his almost-empty mug of cider. I shall not try to reproduce his broad East Anglian accent verbatim, but from what he said, I gathered that the artist in question had been an itinerant who appeared in the village in the 1930s.

"Old Wilf—that was his name. He was nothing more than a tramp," Chris told me. "But according to Joe Stark, who was landlord in those days, he'd done some painting around Colchester and came recommended. So Joe had him do a sign, to replace the old one—which was a grand picture, but a bit worse for wear, though in the end it had to last another ten years.

"I reckon all the pay the tramp got went straight back into the till. He worked hard enough, but all the time he wasn't working he was drinking. It must have rotted his brain over the years, for he used to see things that weren't there. Green mice or pink elephants—you know what I mean. They call it the DTs, don't they? He'd badger anyone who'd listen with tales about the devils and demons who were after him. It wasn't long before people avoided the bar altogether when he was here. Joe Stark's business dropped off, I can tell you; and on the day the painting was finally finished, he was a very happy man.

"If I remember rightly it was later on the self-same day that I was with some of my pals when we saw Wilf running along the street like a madman, shouting, 'Keep it away! Keep it away!' and looking over his shoulder every so often with a terrified expression on his face. You'd have thought Old Nick himself was after him, but none of us saw anything at all. Right outside the church he keeled over and when we got to him, he was dead.

"Well, after that, as you can imagine, Joe decided not to hang up the new sign, especially since it was a very nasty piece of work sure to scare customers away. Must say I'm surprised to hear that you've found the horrible thing after all this time. I thought it had been put on the bonfire long ago."

"It has now," I said. In unison Mrs Miles and I added, "Good riddance to it."

Can the hallucinations created by delirium tremens be so potent that they develop a kind of life of their own? And can that life be transmitted into a two-dimensional copy of one such hallucination? Or conversely, can a man suffering from the DTs somehow imbue the subject of a painting with such vitality that it then pursues him to his grave? After the incidents at Totenhoe, I am inclined to believe that one or the other of the alternatives is a distinct possibility.

There is a small postscript to add to the story. As a result of certain delvings into parish records, I eventually discovered the identity of the tramp, Wilfred Flowerday (a good East Anglian name). Although this in itself is not relevant to my account, I did also find out that the day on which he died was September 15th, 1933. Since Mrs Miles and I destroyed the inn sign on September 15th, nearly fifty years later, the date is clearly significant. I suspect that the strange transformation only took place on the anniversary of the artist's death; in which case it may be that we were the first people 'lucky' enough to see it. I can't say I'm sorry that, by our actions, we have prevented anyone else from sharing our 'luck'. It does leave one obvious, unanswered question though: if we had continued to observe the painting, would the boar have managed to get out?

THE CHAUFFEUR

Courtham House, in its present form, was mostly built during the reigns of Henry the Seventh and his notorious, much-married son; although portions of earlier work are incorporated into its walls. The building is generally considered to be the best Tudor Manor in Cornwall, and since being taken over by the National Trust some years ago, it has become a popular spot with day-trippers. In summer the courtyards and lovely tiered gardens are thronged with holiday-makers; and their cars block the small country lane which runs past Courtham Quay on the River Tamar, and forms the only access to the House. In winter, however, and especially in the evenings, it's a wonderfully lonely and isolated place, despite the fact that Plymouth is no more than fifteen miles away.

My friends Edwin and Marion Farrow live in a rambling cottage attached to, and contemporary with, the main building. It was converted several years ago from two small dwellings, one formerly occupied by the staff chauffeur; and thus the ground-plan is very peculiar and confusing, making it easy to lose oneself when on a visit.

The Farrows are a likeable, middle-aged couple with a quiet sense of humour and a good line in conversation. Edwin is a writer on antiquarian matters, which is how I came to know him. I have an open invitation to stay at Courtham at any time, but until one chilly March about a year ago, I'd had no opportunity to take up the offer. So when I managed to get down to Cornwall for a short holiday, I was determined to spend part of it with Edwin and Marion. In fact, they were kind enough to ask me to stay for the whole week.

My days were devoted to leisurely drives in the surrounding countryside, stopping whenever I came to a church, and sometimes taking photographs for my collection of post-1600 wall paintings. I've been told on many occasions that I miss the most interesting examples by confining myself to those produced after that date, but my response is always that earlier work is well covered by other researchers, and anyway my area of study is just as fascinating, not only historically but artistically too. No one who has seen, for instance, the stunning twentieth-century paintings in Denton church, Northamptonshire, could doubt that. However, this is not the subject of my story. It's so easy to get side-tracked!

Each evening during my holiday, the Farrows

and I would sit snugly around their fragrant log fire—a necessity with the frosty weather we were having then—and enjoy a sherry while we chatted about the places I'd visited that day. One night, just before we started thinking about making a move to go to bed, the subject of ghosts came up.

"Courtham has a ghost, you know," smiled Edwin, "but I'm afraid it is a very traditional one: in the House there is supposed to be a bloodstain which magically appears and disappears on the anniversary of a particularly nasty murder. Unfortunately, as far as anyone knows, there have never been any murders or violent deaths at the Manor; and I for one have never seen the bloodstain! Such stories should definitely be taken with a pinch of salt..."

"But, Jane," interrupted Mrs Farrow, "we must tell you about our very own phantom. It's much more interesting."

"Yes, please," I said, thinking that this wouldn't be very difficult.

"Well, sometimes when I'm in the house on my own," Marion began, "I hear a car drive up and go into our garage—it's the one just outside our gate, by the way; close to where you park your Mini. The first few times it happened, soon after we moved here, I naturally assumed that it was Edwin returning home unexpectedly, but when I went outside to look, there was no one about and the garage was empty.

"Once, I remember, I was sure I heard him come home, and I went to the gate, only to see him drive up, three or four minutes later. I'd begun to think there was something wrong with my hearing, so when Edwin asked why I was waiting for him I made up some silly story about a premonition. He must have wondered whether I'd gone mad!"

"But not long afterwards," her husband added, "I also heard the mysterious noise when I was alone in the cottage and Marion had the car. Since then it has recurred countless times.

"Our theory is that the ghost is Mr Watkins, the old chauffeur who lived here when Courtham was still in private hands. He loved his job so much, and was heartbroken when he had to retire at the age of sixty because of arthritis. He died a few years before we came down here in 1964, so we never knew him, but there are many accounts of his single-minded devotion to work. We think that his death gave him the opportunity to return to his duties in spirit form.

"Your bedroom, Jane, was once part of Mr Watkins' cottage, but nobody has ever seen anything odd or sensed any unnatural atmosphere, either there or in the garage. In fact, one often gets a warm feeling of peace and contentment. If we have a ghost he is obviously very happy, and neither of us would dream of trying to get rid of him. Now I come to think of it though, I haven't heard him for some months now—have you, Marion?"

"No, it's been nearly a year since the last time," Mrs Farrow pondered. "I must admit I miss him..."

The conversation moved on to other topics and shortly afterwards we all went to bed.

* * *

When I awoke next morning, light was pouring in

through the little diamond-paned window in my room. I still felt incredibly tired and an extra half-hour's lie-in seemed very inviting—I didn't even have the energy to check what the time was. It was when I tried to turn over that I became aware of something worse than the normal, early morning lethargy. My limbs felt as though lead weights had been placed on them, and I had an unpleasant feeling of dizziness. I was not even quite sure of my own identity... my one overpowering emotion was of frustration. Whoever I was, I knew that I should be getting up—I had a job of some sort to do, and people were relying on me. However, try as I might I could not move an inch. Then, quite suddenly, the weight lifted and my confusion disappeared along with it.

Over a lone breakfast a little later (the Farrows having already eaten), I tried to account for what had happened to me. I was positive it had not been a dream, and as far as I knew I was not ill: certainly I felt fine now. Could the old chauffeur have been involved? But *how*? Perhaps there was a chance that I might get a clue from his grave, although it seemed unlikely. Still, there could be no harm in paying it a visit, so when Marion came in to see me off on my day's expedition, I asked her where Mr Watkins was buried. As I'd anticipated, it was in Lanstock churchyard, only ten minutes' drive away and the closest village to Courtham. I had already been to the church once, on the previous day, but it would be easy enough to drop in again on my way north to the area on my morning's itinerary.

Lanstock graveyard was larger than I had expected, and finding the tombstone took me some time. Eventually I spotted it—a small grey tablet inlaid with plain black letters. The inscription was unspectacular:

Joseph Watkins
1885–1960
Blessed are the meek

"That doesn't tell me much," I sighed. It had been foolish to hope for an explanation for my strange experience. There was little point in staying, but I remained for a few moments looking at the well-kept plot, with its neatly-cut grass and vase of fresh daffodils wilting slightly in the cold air. "Someone still loves the old man," I thought.

Towards the middle of the grave was a patch of some herb or decorative weed; self-seeded rather than deliberately placed there, by the look of it, but apparently tolerated by the person—a relative?—who tended the plot. I'm no botanist and I couldn't recognise the plant, but its scanty dark green leaves were quite attractive and a little like those of a primrose in shape and texture. Of course, in March there were no flowers to aid identification.

Suddenly I felt driven to bend down and pull out the entire patch by its roots. I was completely unable to control my actions and, almost before I realised what I was doing, there was not a single stem left in the earth. An ugly area of bare soil about ten inches in diameter, and a small pile of uprooted, aromatic herbs at my feet, bore witness to my misdeed. I stepped back, stunned—why had I done such a thing? Normally I would never dream of picking a wild flower, let alone killing it by removing it, root and all, from the ground. That, to me, is unwarrantable vandalism.

Only for a minute did I feel this self-doubt, and then a feeling of satisfaction washed over me. I *had* done the right thing after all. Why, I did not know, but there was a good reason for the removal of the plants. I extracted one from the forlorn pile, wrapped it carefully in tissues and put it into my bag for later identification: if my memory served me right I had seen a small paperback book on herbs in Edwin Farrow's extensive library.

As the day wore on I had other things to think about, including an unseasonable snowstorm which trapped me in Callington church for an hour; and Joseph Watkins and his grave slipped my mind completely. So, at teatime, as I drove through the slush into my usual parking position, tucked around the side of Courtham House, I didn't think twice when I saw Marion Farrow leaning on the cottage gate, looking around with a curious expression on her face.

"You just missed our ghost," she called out, as I waved and went to unload my camera equipment from the boot. Apparently, five minutes earlier she had heard a car driving up and thought it was me, until she realised that the distinctive sound which tyres make as they splash through melting snow was absent.

"It's good to have the old fellow back," she said happily. "I wonder where he's been."

I thought that maybe I knew why the chauffeur had not been about his usual duties, and more than ever I was convinced that I'd acted correctly in taking the herbs from his grave. Now all I needed to do was to name them and discover why they'd had such an effect.

After tea I borrowed Edwin's book on the subject: *British Herbs* by Florence Ranson; and, with some initial difficulty caused by the fact that the book only contained line drawings, I managed to identify the plant with a fair degree of certainty. It was wood betony, and Miss Ranson's description included the following information:

> *...it is... often found around old churches and ruined abbeys. The reason for its cultivation in these places is that it was considered a sure charm against 'evil spirits... and the forces of darkness'.*

It seems that, as well as keeping evil revenants in their graves, betony is capable of restraining good and harmless spirits. After I explained my thoughts to the Farrows they agreed to convince whoever was looking after Mr Watkins' plot that all suspect weeds should be removed as soon as they appeared.

That night and for the rest of my holiday I slept better than I have ever done, and I awoke full of energy. I can't truthfully say that I felt any sort of 'presence' in my bedroom, but there was an atmosphere of peace which had not been there before. My one regret is that I personally did not hear the ghostly car. Perhaps I will be more fortunate next time I go down to Cornwall.

THE HATCHMENT

"What a strange noise that is," I thought as I listened to the sound that the rattling yew tree branches were making in the breeze. "Like dead men's bones—how appropriate for a graveyard."

This poetic if slightly morbid idea came to me one fine, gusty April morning while I sat in the porch outside St Thomas's church, Little Wendens, near Thaxted in north-west Essex. I was waiting for the rector to join me. We had been about to leave the rectory together when the phone had rung and Reverend Swift motioned me to go on ahead of him to the church. Five minutes later, as I was enjoying the peacefulness of the attractive country village, he hurried up with the key for the solid south door of the fourteenth-century building. Once inside we went immediately to the three funeral hatchments in the north aisle. I'd been called in to restore them, and the arrangement was that I should take them back to my house in Oundle for the purpose; so the heavy boards, all approximately forty inches square, had been removed from the wall in readiness.

Hatchments are diamond-shaped wooden panels, usually canvas covered, on which coats of arms, or 'achievements', are painted. They used to be made on the death of the possessor of the arms, then hung outside his or her home during the period of mourning. Later they would usually be rehung in the local church. The custom continued well into the twentieth century, but the examples at Little Wendens were older than this.

On my first visit to the village a few weeks previously, I had made a careful note of the heraldry on each of the hatchments and, after referring to *Papworth's Ordinary of Arms* and to *Burke's Peerage*, I was able, with no small difficulty, to name the bearers of the depicted arms. My identifications agreed with those recorded in the church guide, so I was fairly certain of their accuracy. The three paintings belonged to a former Lord of the Manor and members of his family:

Sir Frederick Bidwell, Bart, lived in Wendens Manor (a building which burned down some years ago) until his death in 1821. On his shield, the Badge of Ulster featured prominently, symbolising his baronetcy; and there was a black and white background, instead of plain black, indicating that his wife had outlived him. The lady in question, Charlotte, eventually died in 1840, and her achievement was in slightly better condition than her husband's. The third lozenge bore the arms of Sir Frederick's younger brother, the Reverend Augustus Bidwell, who passed away in 1823. The Bidwells had obviously followed the custom, common amongst landowning families, of placing their younger son in holy orders: Augustus was the rector of nearby Applestone parish for much of his adult life, until he retired from the incumbency in 1821 to write a theological treatise of characteristic mediocrity.

As Father Swift and I manhandled the boards into my hired van, I mentioned how ironic I thought it was that information was so relatively easy to find about the people for whom hatchments were made, yet the painters themselves were frustratingly anonymous. They rarely signed their works, and churchwardens' accounts usually threw no light on their identity.

"Interesting you should say that," nodded the rector, puffing slightly as he pushed the last canvas into place in the back of the van. "I understand that the painter of these particular achievements *is* known."

As we walked back to the pinkly-pargetted rectory for tea and biscuits before I left for home, he continued: "The village tradition is that old Lady Bidwell painted them. It's said she even made one for herself, a year or two before she died. She was eighty then, you know, but still a proficient amateur artist. I have a little landscape by her in my sitting room; you might like to see it before you go."

Village traditions in general have to be taken

with a very large pinch of salt, but I felt disposed to believe this one. When I examined the Reverend Swift's landscape painting, I was convinced. In the bucolic country scene, with the wooden belfry of Little Wendens church in the distance, I definitely recognised the same hand as that responsible for the hatchments.

The drive home—past the delightful, carved plasterwork fronts so typical of north-west Essex cottages—was a joy, at least to begin with, although I decided none of the houses were as striking as Wendens Rectory itself, with its relief mouldings of sheep, foxes and deer in splendid profusion. I dawdled over the first few miles of the journey. Then the van broke down on the A604 between Cambridge and Huntington, near the Lolworth Turn; and by the time I reached Oundle it was getting late. Unloading the coats of arms and carrying them into my workshop took over an hour, even though the building—a converted garage—is easily accessible. I missed the extra pair of hands which Reverend Swift had provided during the loading. When the unpacking was complete, I was ready for just one thing: a long sleep. Some nine hours later, I awoke duly refreshed and looking forward to the work awaiting me.

A thorough inspection revealed that the hatchment in worst condition was the one belonging to Augustus Bidwell. The canvas needed to be removed from the wooden framework, relined and then re-stretched. I resolved to make that my first job, as the rest of the restoration would be easy by comparison. Progress was slow as

I attempted to take out the heavy nails without damaging the fragile material. After two hours I had completed only one side.

Following a break for coffee I returned to work, noticing as I did so that the temperature in my workshop had dropped markedly. This did not particularly worry me at the time, as it often happened when the wind's direction changed and started blowing through the old warped window.

I was on the point of sitting back down when I saw some dirty grey cobwebs hanging over the edge of the painting near the top. They must have blown there in the draft, I thought. But as I reached to brush them off, they suddenly moved. I realised that they were not cobwebs but hair! Long strands of lank hair were attached to the head of the figure which was now rising up from behind the hatchment.

In a split second I took in the sickly brown face which seemed to have *collapsed in* upon itself, so that the features were hidden beneath loose, dusty wrinkles. Briefly I wondered how I knew that the creature's eyes were piercing and filled with hatred, although I could not actually see them.

Then I was up and making a dash for the door, aware that the figure was also moving, trying to cut me off.

I reached the door and rushed out, pulling it shut behind me, thankful that I'd had a good lock fitted. In the echo of the slam, I heard a heavy sigh which somehow seemed to combine frustration with relief. I listened for several more minutes, not sure what to expect, but with a growing realisation that whatever the thing was, a good lock would not be an effective barrier against it. However, there was no further sound and I began to calm down.

For most of the rest of the day I prowled up and down the house. If I smoked, I would have got through countless cigarettes. Thinking it over, I came to no conclusions as to the identity of the creature. It was female, of that I was sure, though without any real evidence apart from instinct. What connection it had with the Reverend Augustus's memorial I could not fathom. One thing was certain: there was no way I was going to re-enter the workshop on my own.

Finally I decided to drive over to my friend Sally's house in Polebrook, about two miles away. Sally is a very experienced art restorer and a thoroughly down-to-earth individual. If anyone can keep the spooks away, then she's the one to do it. I worked out a credible story about needing her professional help and she agreed to come back with me. By now it was late afternoon. I think she was a little offended and surprised that I didn't offer her coffee before we went along to the workshop; but even with her company I could not face entering it after dusk.

"What exactly is the problem?" Sally asked as we reached the entrance.

"The hatchment canvas is rotting and I'm having trouble getting it off the frame," I replied, manoeuvring her carefully in front of me as I pushed open the door. Looking over her shoulder, I saw that the room appeared to be empty; but, as I followed her in, I felt that the temperature had, if anything, dropped by a few more degrees.

"Let's get down to work then. This is the painting, is it?"

"That's right," I nodded, reluctant to approach it. However, when I had reassured myself that no nightmare figure was lurking anywhere, I joined my friend in prising out the nails.

"You were right to call me in," she muttered. "A job like this needs someone with experience. Why, you're hardly out of art school."

Normally I would have argued light-heartedly with this decidedly inaccurate statement (Sally, at thirty-three, was only five years older than me), but on that day I didn't feel up to it. All the time I sensed something trying to prevent us from removing the canvas, but whatever it was, it seemed powerless to stop us, especially Sally. If several dozen little green men with tentacles had manifested themselves in front of her, she's the type who wouldn't have paused for more than a quick glance.

After an hour or so, we had, between us, removed almost all the nails. As the last one came out, Sally began to ease the hatchment away from its frame.

"That's funny. There are some old sheets of paper tucked behind here, between the frame and the backing board," she said. "Pull them out, will you." Then she looked up suddenly. "I say, you have an extraordinarily noisy cat somewhere close by. It'll be up to no good, I'm sure."

This remark was prompted by an ear-splitting but heartbreaking wailing which had begun as soon as I'd started to pick out the sheets. It sent shivers up my spine, but my companion was unmoved. After a minute or two it faded away into a whispering sob which shortly disappeared altogether.

We laid the painting out carefully and went for a coffee, after which I drove Sally home, then returned as quickly as I could to examine the find. My initial glance had suggested to me that the fewer who knew about the papers, the better it would be, so I was relieved that my friend had assumed they were of no importance.

More detailed examination supported my first impression. The sheets were love letters, six in all: three from the Reverend Augustus Bidwell to his sister-in-law, the Lady Charlotte; and three from Charlotte to her priestly brother-in-law. They were all extraordinarily passionate. I could well imagine the anguish which the couple suffered, caught up in an illicit love affair, ever fearful of discovery. Internal evidence indicated that the affair had lasted for some ten years, from 1789 to 1799. In other words, it began when Charlotte was twenty-nine and her lover slightly younger.

One of the missives, dated December 1799, apparently marked the end of the intimate aspects of the relationship. Lady Bidwell, now middle-aged, vowed eternal devotion although their secret meetings could not continue without her husband finding out. If the couple's mutual feelings continued unabated—and the likelihood is that they did—then the ensuing years must have been difficult ones. When Sir Frederick died, more than twenty years later, there was still no chance of a fairy tale ending to their story. Augustus was forbidden to marry the widow by the Church's Degrees of Marriage, which state that a man may not marry his brother's wife; therefore they would probably have been forced to maintain a facade of mere friendship. Perhaps the pair enjoyed a measure of happiness in each other's company; but even that was swiftly curtailed by the priest's death, which followed all too soon after his brother's decease.

Charlotte was left to a lonely old age. The only way she could think of to record her everlasting adoration was to preserve some of the letters which she and Augustus had exchanged. The peculiar hiding place she chose was her lover's hatchment; a memorial which she herself painted as she mourned his passing.

Her restless spirit, still paying for those years of harmless sin, was evidently afraid that if I found out her guilty secret, I might destroy the record of her tragic love affair. She need not have worried. I replaced the letters when refitting the newly-lined canvas, and told no one of the discovery. At one stage I considered confiding in the Reverend Swift, but decided against such a course. His modern, rational brand of Christianity would probably have taken no account of ghosts.

I do sometimes wonder whether I did the right thing. If I had severed Charlotte Bidwell's one remaining attachment to the physical world, by burning the papers, she might now be resting more easily. I suppose I can console myself with the thought that I did what she would have wanted me to do. I don't think that can be wrong, can it?

THE WANDLEBURY
EYECATCHER

At three o'clock I was expected in Little Bington, eight miles south-east of Cambridge, to finalise arrangements for some restoration work which I was shortly to begin on an early perpendicular screen in the church; and, in my usual way I had departed from my home in Northamptonshire rather early, to allow for possible delays during the drive down. However, since none of the anticipated problems materialised, I found when I arrived in Cambridge that I had a great deal of time to kill. A snack in Trinity Street disposed of half an hour most pleasantly, but as I left the outskirts of the city I knew that I would still reach my destination with an hour to spare unless I stopped somewhere on the way.

A couple of minutes later a faded signpost loomed up on the left, indicating that I was approaching a side-road leading to 'Wandlebury Village and Church Only'.

"I might as well while away some time looking in the church," I thought, as I turned down the narrow, bumpy lane; mentally keeping my fingers crossed that I would not find locked doors when I got there.

The lane curved gently for about a mile then, just outside the village, with the church tower visible in the distance, I noticed something partly hidden in a copse at the side of the road. It seemed, as I passed, to be the ruins of some sort of old building, and I was sufficiently intrigued to stop the car and reverse to a convenient parking place. As I left the Mini and started walking through the trees towards the masonry, I saw that my first impression had been slightly inaccurate. Here were no ancient remains but instead an unusual and picturesque folly: a sham ruin erected perhaps two hundred years ago, no doubt as an eyecatcher to enhance the view from a nearby manor house. The structure which I made out through the undergrowth took the form of a long and carefully irregular wall of knapped flint, roughly twenty feet high in the middle and tapering to half that at the sides. It was pierced in three places by pointed arches; the central and largest one of which was open, and framed a view of the countryside behind it, unaccountably drained of bright colour, or so it appeared to me. Shivering a little, and telling myself to stop imagining things I turned my attention to the other two arches, both of which looked as though they must once have led into small rooms. The left-hand one had, however, been recently and crudely blocked up, and I noticed with regret that the same fate was evidently in store for the other, judging from the bricks piled untidily by it.

No-one was at work there at the moment though, and the area seemed quite deserted, so I succumbed to temptation and clambered over the ugly wire fence which encircled the ruin and barred my way. Approaching the right-hand arch I found that, as I expected, it formed the entrance to a room: a plain rectangle about ten feet by eight, without decoration of any sort to relieve its harshness. I took a step inside, avoiding a dead starling lying on the floor, and wrinkled my nose at the unpleasant smell which probably indicated an infestation of rodents, although I could not shake off the notion that the stones themselves were exuding it.

Without a doubt this was the most repulsive and depressing folly I had ever seen, and I was just deciding to go when I heard a movement. Despite the bright sunshine outside, the light did not penetrate to the far corners of the room, and it was from one of these that I thought I detected the stirrings of something rather large and heavy. This was puzzling for, black as the corners were, the darkness was too limited in area to conceal anything bigger than a rabbit or a small dog. Yet no animal of that size could have made the sound I had heard. I took another step forward, peering through the gloom, but when I realised that the ground was trembling perceptibly under my feet, I very quickly lost interest. Suddenly I felt an irresistible urge to leave for more peaceful surroundings.

I hurried back to the car, which seemed a long way away, and drove down the road to the church. This proved to be a medium-sized, late medieval building: nothing out of the ordinary, but in my present mood, that was all to the good. I was further reassured by the satisfyingly normal sight of three ladies busily arranging flowers in the chancel. They were being supervised by a fourth: a tall person of mature years who, when she saw me examining the monuments in the nave, came over and introduced herself as the vicar's wife, Mrs Parry. I made the mistake of explaining about the work I was due to start nearby and, for my sins, spent the next fifteen minutes answering a seemingly endless stream of questions about various hatchments, monuments and paintings which needed cleaning or restoration. Only after I had dealt with all her queries was I able to bring the talkative Mrs Parry around to the subject of the folly.

"Oh, you mean the 'Wandlebury Eyecatcher'," she said with a slight frown. "Well, Miss Bradshaw, I'm afraid it's rather a sore point with us at the moment. It was built by Sir John Crawshay in the 1770s to be seen from Crawshay Hall; which was burned down in the last century by the way. The villagers have somehow acquired a number of ridiculous ideas about him: it *is* true that he knew Sir Francis Dashwood and was a frequent visitor to West Wycombe, but one must be charitable. There is no evidence that he was anything more than a rich and decadent eccentric, especially since his friendship with Dashwood wasn't formed until the later and, I understand, less excessive days of the so-called Hell-Fire Club, after Sir Francis had given up Medmenham Abbey. Sir John's doubtful character has been exaggerated and blackened out of all recognition by the people around here—for instance he is supposed to have gambled with the Devil and lost... Yes, I can see what you're thinking: that it isn't exactly the most uncommon of stories; and you're right of course, but our version has an original twist."

Sitting down in a pew, and after an aside about her rheumatism, she resumed, "When Sir John lost his bet, the Devil is said to have trapped his soul for eternity in the folly. The old folk would have you believe that it is very dangerous to enter one of the 'eyes' at night; 'eyes' are the name they give to those two small rooms on either side of the main arch, incidentally. Every so often, they say, Sir John requires a victim (why, is not explained) and if you are foolish enough to visit the folly by night your body is likely to be discovered the following morning, quite dead and with its face set in an awful grimace of terror.

"My husband and I have done our best to convince them that the entire story is a fabrication deriving from a misunderstanding of the word 'Eyecatcher', but naturally they think they know better. Unfortunately, their beliefs have received support lately, in most tragic circumstances. A few weeks ago a tramp wandered into one of the 'eyes' to shelter from a storm, and died there. He was an elderly chap and suffered, it seems, from heart trouble, so when he passed on in his sleep there was really no mystery. This hasn't stopped the parishioners from doing their best to make a mystery out of it though, and some have managed a little mild hysteria too. A group of them has even decided to brick up the 'eyes'. I expect you noticed that one is now blocked?"

I nodded and Mrs. Parry paused for breath and continued. "We have tried to stop this, as it's such a shame to spoil a rare old building for the sake of superstition, but they are quite determined and there is nothing we can do."

Secretly I agreed with the locals, but there was no point in arguing with the lady so I made the appropriate sympathetic noises. Anyway the time was getting on, and I took my leave shortly afterwards, in the knowledge that if I delayed any longer I would be late for my appointment. However, when I had driven out of the village, I stopped the Mini again, persuading myself that I could spare a minute or two for just one last look at the folly. I suppose I was hoping that my initial repulsion would prove to have been ill-founded, but as soon as I entered the copse I knew that something was still very wrong with the place. "And no Birds Sing," I thought, quoting the title of an E.F. Benson story; for certainly there were no birds, not even the ubiquitous wood pigeon, in the surrounding trees. I reached the wire fence and was about to climb over when I noticed that the ruin looked somehow different. It took a few seconds to fathom out what had happened, and then the light dawned: the left-hand archway, which had been blocked up, was now open again, and the new bricks were strewn about over the ground for a distance of several yards. The inside of the 'eye' thus revealed was black as pitch, and nothing stirred there, but I'm afraid this did little to comfort me.

It definitely did not seem like a good idea to investigate further; and after all, I *did* have my appointment to keep, so I felt justified in going no closer. As I returned to the car I found it increasingly hard to maintain a nonchalant facade: I would like to claim that I managed to resist the impulse to break into a run, but I suspect an observer, had there been one, would disagree with me!

Some weeks later I received a request from the rector of Wandlebury to undertake the restoration in his church, but I'm ashamed to say that I pleaded pressure of work in order to avoid going back to the area. There are, I think, some buildings which are deeply and dangerously bad. Whether or not Wandlebury Eyecatcher obtained its evil nature by the actions of Sir John Crawshay, in the way the villagers believe, is a question no one can answer now; although I did discover recently that exactly the same story was current over a hundred and fifty years ago when another unfortunate vagrant was found dead within an 'eye'. Of one thing I am quite certain however: that nothing could ever persuade me to go near the monstrous folly again, let alone enter one of its 'eyes'.

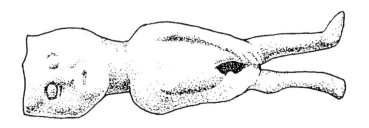

THE SHEELAGH-NA-GIG

When William Haydn became rector of the parish of Applestone, a little village a few miles from Thaxted in the rural part of Essex close to the borders with Cambridgeshire and Hertfordshire, he quickly realised that the inside of the small fourteenth-century church, complete with timber belfry, was badly in need of repair. In particular, the rood screen, with its pretty tracery, and two late seventeenth-century monuments, were covered with the grime of many years, obscuring what appeared (to his admittedly untrained eye) to be their original colouring.

William's plan to have the furnishings restored easily gained the support of the parishioners, the female half of whom were won over by his youthful enthusiasm and good looks. Even the men admitted that, in twenty years or so, when he wasn't such a newcomer, the young priest would make a good replacement for the former rector, recently deceased. The ladies were full of money-making schemes, from bring-and-buy sales to sponsored bike races for the children. There was also the likelihood of a 'top-up' grant from an august body, so paying for the work would be little problem, though William was soon sick and tired of the formalities and paperwork involved. I think he was relieved, therefore, when I, the restorer recommended by the Diocesan Advisory Board, arrived at Applestone to spend a couple of days at the rectory and do some preliminary tests in the church.

It was just after Christmas, and pretty chilly, but at least it wasn't snowing as I drew up my red Mini in front of the rectory as dusk started to fall. Of course, no work could be done that night, but the rector met me at the car and insisted on helping me to unload the cleaning materials and carry them over to the church right away. I knew the signs: here was a cleric so excited about his new living that he would insist on giving me the guided tour immediately, and no plea of a tiring journey would deter him. Best to get it over and done with; and, anyway, churches at dusk have their own particular atmosphere which has always appealed to me.

Some forty-five minutes later, having made approving and admiring noises about everything in the building that William Haydn pointed out to me (which did, indeed, seem like everything), I stood outside the church, waiting while he carefully locked the door. In the silence, my stomach rumbled embarrassingly, reminding me that I had not eaten since breakfast. I hoped that whoever cooked the meals at the rectory had been told that I was vegetarian.

Although by then it was quite dark, I could still make out most of the details of the church's exterior, and one thing in particular caught my eye. Under the eaves, to the east of the porch, was as fine an example of a sheelagh-na-gig stone carving as I had ever seen. These rather gross symbols of female sexuality, usually depicted as a naked, pregnant, and very busty woman, holding open her genitalia, are quite rare, and no one really knows what they represent. In most cases, I tend to favour the prosaic explanation that they are charms to protect the church against being struck by lightning.

I made some remark about the sheelagh-na-gig to William as he joined me, and noted with amusement that he was blushing fetchingly, if somewhat anachronistically.

Mrs Chapman, the housekeeper, served me with a pleasant mushroom omelette for supper, though she made it evident that such a meagre repast wouldn't do for the rector, who instead had a large plate of chops. There was a further hiccup in our relationship when Mrs Chapman said, "I've got a nice bit of fish for you tomorrow, Miss Bradshawe," and I had to explain that vegetarians don't eat fish. Nevertheless, the good inroads I made into the apple pie she provided for pudding seemed to improve her mood considerably.

Feeling replete, I settled down with coffee,

while William searched through his bookshelves for something. Eventually he found it and handed it to me, saying, "I'm afraid this is the only published history of the parish, but it's not without interest."

L.G. Beddoes's *History and Antiquities of Applestone* (privately printed in 1907) proved to be rather charmingly filled with line drawings of the village; drawings which might be better described as enthusiastic rather than skilful. Here, for instance, was a picture of the sheelagh-na-gig.

"Look at this," I said. "It doesn't look a lot like the real thing, does it?"

"Now you mention it," the priest replied, "you're right. I suppose Beddoes' artistic abilities weren't quite up to it."

"I think there's probably more to it than that," I said. "The differences between this and the actual carving are mainly of only one kind. The artist has toned down the sexuality of the original: see, the stomach is slimmer and the legs are not spread so far apart. This is nothing more than a fine example of Victorian prudishness. Beddoes may have been writing six years after Queen Victoria's death, but nineteenth-century morality didn't die with the turn of the century."

"That's really fascinating," said the rector, squirming a little. I quickly realised that nineteenth-century morality was still alive in the 1990s, especially among young men who had gone from public school straight into theological college, and had probably never had a girlfriend.

I should have slept well. The location was certainly perfect. Applestone Rectory is two hundred years old, and adorned with delightful pargetting—that plasterwork decoration which is so common in north-west Essex. It is a particularly fine example, with patterns, flowers, and the occasional pink sheep and fox frolicking joyfully across the front of the house. What's more, the inside of the building has been carefully modernised, and my bedroom even had a bathroom en suite. I have stayed in everything from hideously drafty Victorian monstrosities to the tiny 'executive homes' which often replace them. If only all rectories could be like this one, I thought.

But sleep was slow in coming and, on the edge of it, I had to endure more than the usual number of hypnogogic dreams, which took the standard form of a familiar shape slowly transforming itself into something hideous. I have often thought that the scene in M.R. James's 'A View from a Hill', where a perfectly ordinary arm rises out of the ground and then begins to grow "hairy and dirty and thin", must have been based on a hypnogogic dream of Monty's. Mine at Applestone, though, mostly concerned the sheelagh-na-gig, sometimes as portrayed by Beddoes, sometimes as it was in reality, and sometimes even grosser than that.

Nevertheless, I woke in a good mood, and started work in the church straight after breakfast. The morning passed uneventfully, but when I returned to the rectory for lunch I found that William had a visitor. Every village has its local historian, who likes to think of himself (or, indeed, herself) as the sole reservoir of accurate knowledge on the area. Mr Harvey was Applestone's. Apparently he had decided that I would need to see his huge collection of old photographs of the church in order to do my work properly. Not that I had any real objections to this—I like old photos as much as anyone, and they can be a valuable source of information—but I knew that I would need to get back to the church as soon as possible to take advantage of the light before it started to fail.

It was only polite to have a quick glance through the pictures, though I almost skipped straight past it when I came upon the sheelagh-na-gig photograph, but something odd struck me. Yes, there was no doubt about it: the carving in the picture differed from its present form. The female figure was distinctly less gross. By no means as decorous as in Beddoes' drawing, but not so fat as she was now. The photograph was, I noticed, dated on the back: 1945. Perhaps my dreams of the previous night had pre-disposed me to this revelation, but somehow I did not feel terribly surprised. Racking my brains for an explanation, however, produced only a—not terribly useful—memory of Walter de la Mare's '*All Hallows*', in which evil forces progressively alter and restore a cathedral according to their own design.

Presumably whatever transformation had taken place had happened so slowly that no one in the village had noticed. Mr Harvey might have spotted it, since he apparently knew every single detail of every one of his photographs, but questioning revealed that he was severely short-sighted, and had not been able to see the original carving for years. In the face of the inexplicable, it's probably always the best idea to get on with the mundane, so

I returned to work that afternoon and quite forgot the sheelagh-na-gig in my preoccupation with the cleaning tests on the monuments, which confirmed my suspicions that the colouring was almost certainly contemporary, though retouched at a later date.

The next day I expected to complete my assignment, but meanwhile that evening, with nothing to do, I returned to pondering on the mystery. Given William's response on the previous two occasions when the sheelagh-na-gig had been mentioned, I decided not to raise the subject with him and, as a result, conversation tended to flag after supper. In the end, he suggested a visit to the local public house, and I happily agreed.

The Green Man seemed a pleasant enough country pub, although I noticed with some irritation that the inn sign depicted a very ordinary Robin Hood instead of a portrayal of what some say is an ancient fertility symbol (the male version of the sheelagh-na-gig, I recalled, but quickly put that thought from my mind).

I was introduced to Johnny Fryer, the village gossip and storehouse of local stories for the past sixty years. I'm not quite sure how, but, despite my best efforts, the conversation came around to the subject of the stone hag; or "Nagging Sheila", as Johnny called her.

"They did used to say," he chuckled, "that she were an old goddess who the vicar had trapped in the stone and wouldn't let out. My old grandparents would take a pear or apple or somesuch every year at Harvest Festival time and put it down by the wall under her, instead of in the church. A lot of other folks did the same. Us young 'uns thought it were all very silly, but we did get a beating if we tried to take some of the fruit, so it were left to rot. Do you notice when you go to the church tomorrow how good the ground is there for growing things."

The codger paused for a drink (he could see that I was really interested, in spite of myself, and reckoned I'd be good for another pint at least). "No one puts fruit out for her nowadays, but if you can believe the story I heard from my old gaffer then perhaps we oughta. Grandpa Fryer used to say that, while Sheila herself could never get free, she were pregnant, and if people stopped giving her her due, she'd get angry and eventually have a baby who'd take over the world. He said there were a bit in the Bible about it—Revelations, it were."

William, who had just come up and was listening pink-facedly to the conversation, opened his mouth to correct him, but Johnny wasn't going to let anyone interrupt his tale, especially now that he'd reached the punchline.

"Some do say that the Sheila is growing and getting bigger and bigger with child, though I don't see it myself."

"That really is quite enough," burst out the rector. "Don't you believe a word of it, Jane—he's the best story-teller in East Anglia."

As we walked back to the rectory, William broke the silence.

"I hope you didn't let what Johnny said worry you. He really is a great liar; or maybe it would be more charitable to call him an embroiderer of facts."

I was less sure about that, but the rector was hardly the right person to discuss it with. I made some comment about there possibly being a basis of truth in Johnny's story, and if so it was a remarkably late survival of goddess worship, and left it at that.

I left it at that over breakfast the next morning too. In fact, I was so taciturn that Mrs Chapman took offence and clearly decided that her initial impression of me had been the correct one after all. I desperately wanted to complete my work in Applestone and get away as soon as possible. The whole village had taken on a nightmare quality. Whatever was happening, there was nothing I could do about it, and I felt that if only I could leave, I would return to the real world. I had already decided that, were I to be offered the full restoration job, I would find some reason to refuse it.

But my best-laid plans to avoid looking at the sheelagh-na-gig when I returned to the church to finish up came to nothing. As I passed it, I was unable to resist a swift glance in its direction.

In a way it was a relief, as I had almost expected it, although if Johnny Fryer's stories were even half true, the consequences don't bear thinking about. The sheelagh-na-gig had been transformed. It was no longer a grotesque female caricature. The new carving was crude and unformed, but there was no question about it... now it portrayed the Madonna and Child.

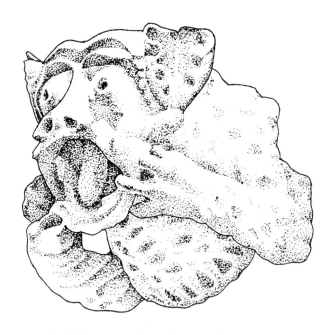

THE CAMBRIDGE BEAST

Night climbing—which is simply the scaling of historic buildings under cover of darkness, with no other motive besides excitement and the love of challenge—has been a popular pursuit amongst students at Cambridge for at least a hundred years; although, interestingly, Oxford does not seem to have the same tradition.

Despite its long history, I like to think that we ourselves were the first all-female group to tackle the sport with any seriousness. My name is Penny Cole and my companions were Jackie Pearson, Heather Philpott and Sarah Lyford. We had come up to Cambridge at the same time in the early 'seventies, and were all members of New Hall. Our subjects ranged from natural sciences to divinity so we were not naturally thrown together, but within a few months of our arrival at college we had met, discovered a mutual interest in mountaineering, and determined to try our hand at the night climbing about which we had heard so much. Luckily we were all very fit, and what Jackie and I lacked in height (we were, and are, both under five foot two) was made up for in stamina and determination, although there is no denying that our missing inches did rule out a few climbs.

If anyone could be said to have been our leader, it was Sarah, who usually took the initiative on our ascents and would always be first to try a difficult manoeuvre. The rest of us were practical souls who loved adventure but had no intention of breaking our necks experiencing it. We never really understood Sarah's extreme 'live for today' attitude, although we were all very fond of her in spite of this (it was noticeable that her philosophy did not extend beyond herself—with us she was often quite the opposite and we frequently likened her to a mother hen with her chicks!)

For a year we had a great time, tackling most of the classic climbs (the Old Schools, St John's Chapel and so on) with considerable success; but after our attempt on King's College Chapel we all lost interest and drifted apart. The details of this climb have never been broadcast beyond our group, but for reasons which I shall explain later, I feel that now is the time to make them public.

In the mid-1930s, concrete blocks—so much more effective than spikes—were placed at strategic points on the Chapel walls, thereby making impossible the traditional route up the building (which students since the last century had enjoyed). However, this only served to stimulate the ingenuity of the climbers, who were soon finding different (if harder) ways up. In 1965 several students managed to erect a huge 'Peace in Vietnam' banner high between the two east pinnacles which overlook King's Parade; thus causing much consternation and a certain amount of glee amongst tourists and college authorities alike. Their account was written up by 'Hederatus' in his book on *Cambridge Night Climbing*, and since then other groups have tended to follow the same route: up the north wall of the Chapel to the roof, and then on to any of the four pinnacles.

After a year we felt that we were ready to attempt that most exciting of Cambridge climbs—exciting not only because of its severity but also because the Chapel in some way seems to symbolise the whole city: it is the quintessence of all that is Cambridge, and thus the climber who conquers it feels afterwards that *anything* is within their capacity.

Naturally we examined the building carefully by daylight before the ascent, and although we did our best to look like interested tourists, it was hard to maintain a nonchalant facade as our excitement grew. In an effort to relieve the tension, I remember that I pointed up as we surveyed the north-west corner, and commented on the King's Beasts—those assorted heraldic animals (the badges of Henry VIII and his ancestors) which bedeck the walls of the Chapel.

"Maybe they come alive at night," I said jokingly. "I'd quite like to meet a dragon!"

"You never knew my old headmistress, did

you?" said Jackie, and we all laughed.

* * *

The night we chose for our climb was a perfect one in the Easter Term, during a break between exams. We waited impatiently until 1:30am before leaving our rooms, armed with ropes and other necessary equipment, including the appropriate footwear. Everything was quiet when we reached King's shortly afterwards, so with as few preliminaries as possible, we started up the north face. As usual Sarah led the way, and we followed her to the lower roof with no particular problems. The 'second stage', as it were, was much tougher, and when Sarah reached the top—the main Chapel roof—and secured the rope, she called down softly that she thought a long stretch to a drainpipe above the window would be too much for Jackie and me, since we were so short. Naturally, a number of rather unladylike words passed our lips at this point, but we were determined not to give up so easily. We decided that Heather should go up next: being only a couple of inches taller than us, she would be able to judge the necessary reach better than our near-six-foot leader.

She had mounted no more than ten feet when we heard a loud scream from above her, and Sarah came rushing over the parapet down towards us, abseiling with such speed that I was sure she must fall or at least put a foot through the priceless stained glass window. However, she reached us safely, although I'm certain that, if Heather had not moved quickly out of the way, she would have been knocked for six.

As Sarah landed on the lower roof beside us, the most disgusting smell I have ever experienced came wafting down from somewhere above. If you can imagine the stink of the abattoir, multiplied tenfold, you will have a rough idea of its effect. Trying to prevent myself from retching, I looked at Sarah and saw that she had a line of slight, red scratches on one cheek.

"What happened?" I cried.

"No time! Let's get out of here," she shouted, already heading towards the edge of the roof.

We needed no encouragement. The smell was obnoxious enough to drive anyone away; and in addition, to judge from ominous noises below us, Sarah's scream had attracted the attention of a passing policeman out on King's Parade. We made our escape over the Chapel lawns and along the Backs, thus managing to avoid the minion of the law who, miraculously, seemed to be looking for us in quite the wrong place.

It was sometime later that a rather grimy and puzzled quartet sat around drinking coffee in my room at New Hall. After a slightly awkward silence, Jackie spoke for the three of us when she said: "Now, Sarah, will you tell us what's going on?"

Sarah sighed. "I suppose you must know..." She seemed to steel herself before continuing. "It was when I shone my torch over the roof towards the east—I saw this thing coming towards me, no more than three or four yards away. It was maggotty white and very like an enormous dog, crawling along on its belly. I'll tell you what it reminded me of most: that greyhound in the King's Beasts which you pointed out the other day, Penny. And just as if it was made of stone, it was sort of eaten-away and decayed, although it had terrible yellow teeth and claws. The smell was revolting, like something from a graveyard; and I was nearly sick. Then the animal seemed to spring at me, and I felt it touch my face. I just dropped my torch (which I have *no* intention of going back for) and ran for my life. You know the rest."

We had expected to hear something strange, but this encounter was quite beyond us, and although we talked about it until well past dawn, an acceptable explanation eluded us. I think it was Heather who finally suggested that the creature might have been some sort of large crippled bird. Remembering that noxious smell, which even now—despite careful washing—seemed to linger in the scratches on Sarah's cheek, we knew deep down that this could not possibly be the answer, but it was the only one we had, so we welcomed it with open arms. It did occur to me that the animal's resemblance to one of the King's Beasts might not be coincidence, and that the restoration currently in progress on some of the carvings on the south wall of the Chapel might have awakened something which should have been left undisturbed; but this smacked too much of the occult and Masonic secrets for my liking, and I did not mention it to my companions, although I suspect that Sarah at least would have taken it seriously.

At any rate, in the following months we set about the nearly impossible task of forgetting all about it.

Although her physical scars healed, Sarah never recovered her 'devil-may-care' outlook on life, and despite making a game effort to keep up her academic work, she only received the 'consolation prize' of an ordinary degree. I believe she is now a wife and mother somewhere in the West Midlands. The rest of us obtained our Honours BAs, and went on to further research in our various fields. I myself have just begun two years of post-doctoral work at Cambridge.

I don't suppose I had thought of Sarah and our night climbing activities for many months, until recently a banner headline on the front-page of the *Cambridge Evening News* caught my eye and brought back memories of unpleasant vividness: 'STUDENT KILLED IN CLIMB ON KING'S COLLEGE CHAPEL', it read. Apparently, William Harrison (aged 20), a 'brilliant student' of Trinity, had slipped while climbing the north side of the Chapel, and fallen to the ground, where he was discovered early next morning with a broken neck. Police were puzzled by deep gashes on his face which made him almost unrecognisable. It was assumed that they had been obtained during his fall or on impact. The newspaper report ended with a stern warning against night climbing, referring to a similar fatality six months previously (which I had missed, being in London finishing my PhD at the time).

I have given a great deal of thought to this in the past few days, and I do not believe that the marks on William Harrison's face were caused by his fall. Perhaps Sarah Lyford avoided the same fate only because whatever is up there on the roof was weaker then, and still ill-formed. How the thing is gaining strength I do not know, but l am very much afraid that one day, not too far in the future, it will be strong enough to come down from its lair. I hope I am no longer in Cambridge if and when that happens.

But I can't help wondering whether the beast is the only one of its kind; are there other old buildings which harbour similar beings in forgotten nooks and crannies? If so, nowhere will be safe should they choose to make their existence known.

Printed in Great Britain
by Amazon